PLANET OF PERIL

Trouble came early!

A whole legion of crab-rats was advancing from the direction of the swamp. By midday hundreds of the fearsome creatures had moved into the area and were sunning themselves in the open spaces Bogaert and Zim had so laboriously cleared.

Any single creature was fully a match for an armed man . . . and the horrific tide-now surrounded the pod completely.

Effectively, the humans were besieged.

Some of the crab-rats were even investigating the close-by rocky outcrop, as if considering the site appropriate for a nest.

And if that weren't bad enough, a large group waited impatiently near the pod . . . attracted by the scent of human flesh inside!

Also by Colin Kapp:

PATTERNS OF CHAOS
THE WIZARD OF ANHARITTE

THE SURVIVAL GAME

Colin Kapp

BALLANTINE BOOKS • NEW YORK

All rights reserved under International and Pan-American Copyright Conventions. Published in the United States by Ballantine Books, a division of Random House, Inc., New York, and simultaneously in Canada by Ballantine Books of Canada, Ltd., Toronto, Canada.

Library of Congress Catalog Card Number: 76-11820

ISBN 0-345-25192-X-150

Manufactured in the United States of America

First Edition: September 1976

Cover art by H. R. Van Dongen

THE SURVIVAL GAME

ONE

Evening cupped blood-red hands around the city of Tenarensor. The quaint towers of the capital of Ortel became less distinct as the yellow sky darkened through maroon to a deep crimson, shot with the bright stars of the Hub. In mounting chorus the bright horns called over the rooftops, summoning the faithful to give thanks to the gods and call blessings on Oontara, the star king, whose imperious grip on more than a hundred habitable worlds kept the trade lanes free around the Hub and assured the vast fortunes of the empire.

Inside the palace, the twirling shadows of the triple suns at last found rest in the motionless crimson of night. A capricious breeze dallied with the ornate drapes, penetrating the window frets and disturbing the priceless fabrics around the gaming table. Star King Oontara watched the result of its antics, a little surprised, and turned to his guest.

"My Lord Xzan is cold, perhaps?"

Seated at the gaming table between two windows, each of which contributed its fiery glow to the villainous outline of his face, the visiting star lord could adequately have personified the principal of some ancient demonolatry.

"My dear Oontara, you grow soft on this torrid world of yours. I've said so before. I mind when you could wage great battles with the blood cold as ice in your veins. Yet now you're disturbed by the merest draft."

"I was thinking only of your comfort, Xzan. I welcome a breath of fresh air."

"Maybe. But I repeat, you're going soft. What use is it for a star king to ply trade with Terra?"

"Oh, so that's what's been on your mind all evening!" Oontara set about stacking new tokens on the gaming table. "And I thought you'd tried too much of the wine, or too few of the women. We sadly misjudge each other, old comrade."

"We used not. We were a fair match in cunning and guessing."

"Nothing's changed. There's still no matter in which I can't equal or better you. As for your opinions of Terra, they're born of ignorance."

With a deft movement of his hand, Oontara spread the gaming tokens across the board, each one falling with mathematical precision. The gesture was not lost on Xzan, who attempted to follow suit but failed.

"Is this what Terran influence has reduced you to—a gamesmaster?" asked Xzan critically. "Those who consort with the weak themselves become weaker."

"You think Terra's weak?"

"The Terrans are a race of weaklings. There's scarcely one I couldn't destroy with a single hand. And none I couldn't tear apart with two."

"Physically that may be true, but you've forgotten the strength of their technology. If you want to see controlled power in action, you should see my Terran-built bark. It's the most singular ship in space."

"I've heard of your ingenious toy. History proves innovators count for little when faced with trained arms. Come, Oontara! You and I have the empires to prove it. Would you pit a Terran expeditionary force against a legion of hereditary star warriors? Of course not."

"Since you answer your own questions, you presumably don't want to hear my views," said Oontara silkily.

"Heh! It was the *ransad,* the old knowledge, which carved the parsecs off the galaxy and made the star empires possible. That was a thousand years before the infant Terrans even discovered the wheel. All their technology's won for them is eight habitable planets—all of them self-governed. They don't even have the strength to rule what they've gained. I give such playthings to favored concubines."

"You're trying to make me angry, Xzan." Oontara bent low over the table, examining the geometrical designs. "You'll not succeed. You've already shown your hand."

"I have?" Xzan's evil visage scanned the game and found nothing amiss, then looked up to meet Oontara's crafty smile.

"Yes. You thought Oontara's flirtation with Terra so unlikely, you had to come in person to find out what the star fox was up to. You felt impelled to know what advantage Oontara could gain from Terra which might be to your detriment. Aren't I right?"

"I admit a certain curiosity."

"Had you asked me direct, I'd have told you. I've seen the light."

"The light?" Xzan's hand faltered on the board, and he misplaced a minor token, but dared not withdraw.

"Certainly!" Oontara saw the false move and was heartened by it. "We were taught that the *ransad* was absolute—that nothing further could ever be known. The Terrans have proved that knowledge is unending. Whatever you know is only a steppingstone to the infinite possibilities of what could be known. Already they can step a tenth of the way to the next galaxy. Why be limited to this one alone when the universe contains more galaxies than the Milky Way does stars?"

Xzan was dubious. "You haven't mentioned price. What do these wonders cost?"

"Merely the promise to assume membership in the Galactic Federation."

"Federation!" Xzan's scorn was terrible. "Once there were no laws around the Hub but my word and your word, my whim and your whim. That has been the way of star kings since time began. Yet you seek an alliance with upstart weaklings, and talk of federation. I can hear the gods laughing from here."

"The alliance serves me well. I've access to technology the *ransad* said couldn't exist. And if the promise of my plans is fulfilled, I'll one day control a million worlds where now I've but a hundred. Even Kam Kanizar, the King of Kings, will sit at my feet."

Xzan spat expressively at the immaculate drapes. "In a federation you'll control nothing. In return, you'll have lost your warrior's soul. You're selling your birth-right for a handful of platitudes and a headful of ideas."

"You speak as if there were a choice in the matter. There isn't, Xzan. Our way of life became extinct the day Terra independently discovered hyperdrive."

"What sort of heresy is this?"

"No heresy—a revelation. We've been worshipping false gods."

"Mine are the gods of strength and terrible vengeance. Show me anything in the universe stronger than these."

"I intend to. He's a little, fat Terran by the name of Hilary Rounding—Commissioner for Terran Outspace Technical Aid. Neither you nor your gods stand a chance against him."

Oontara reached for a golden tassel, which evoked a distant, soulful bell. A servant appeared, approaching with the deep, obsequious bows which the presence of star nobility demanded.

"Tell the Commissioner we'll be pleased to see him now."

The man who entered made no attempt to follow protocol. He strode into the room with a broad smile and a hand ready for shaking. Oontara had described him as a little, fat Terran. He could have added that Rounding was bald, suntanned, and seemingly unaware of the awe in which star nobility was held.

Xzan regarded the white-clad dumpling with much surprise, and shook the proffered hand before he had time to consider what the salutation meant. His reaction to the soft, fleshy skin was one of considerable distaste. He looked at Oontara appealingly. If this was the star king's idea of someone who could depose the ancient gods and draw the teeth of hereditary legions, then Oontara had indeed gone soft.

"Lord Oontara, Lord Xzan," the jovial Terran was saying, "I'd like to introduce a colleague of mine— Colonel Bogaert, known to the rest of the universe as Colonel Bogey." He waved his hand toward the door, and a second Terran entered. "Bogey's my technical and military aide. You warlike chaps should find a lot in common."

While Rounding had been speaking, his eyes had been active, noting the devillike scowl of Xzan with a questing interest. Xzan had the uncomfortable feeling that the fat Terran was reading a lot more from his face than the star lord wanted him to know. The arrival of the second Terran served to divert the unwelcome attention.

Colonel Bogaert was as unlike his superior as could be imagined. He was tall and lean, with muscles hard from a lifetime in the Space Service. The spring in his step hinted at an internal confidence not explained entirely by his fitness as a military man. Like most Terran Service technicians, he was quiet-spoken, yet there was an edge of command at the back of his voice which gave his casual words more than ordinary force. Xzan sensed that here was a man who held a great deal in reserve.

Even so, Colonel Bogey was not to Xzan's liking. He had neither the swaggering superiority of a hereditary warrior nor the desperate cunning of the professional survivor. Xzan summed him up as a "painted warrior,"—a derogatory term used around the Hub to describe those who used a show of arms without true appreciation of the realities of battle.

Oontara read his guest's disapproval with shrewd eyes, and turned to the Colonel.

"As a military man, Colonel Bogaert, you've surely acquired knowledge of our war game. Have a look at our play, and tell me what you think of Xzan's position."

Bogaert gave the board a few minutes' deep consideration.

"Indefensible, of course. My Lord Xzan would be advised to surrender before his losses became insupportable."

"What!" Xzan rose swiftly to the defense. "My vocabulary admits no such word as 'surrender.'"

"Does it have a term for complete annihilation?" asked Bogaert quietly.

"The concept exists—for application to enemies and weaklings."

"But not for yourselves?"

"You're bluffing, Colonel. The game's still open."

"Yet can be won by a single move."

"What's that?" Oontara crossed to the board with some surprise. "If I've victory, I've yet to see its form."

"You don't have victory. But there's a move that could assure it."

"Which?"

Bogaert turned from the board with a slightly apologetic smile. "I fear to spoil the game for my Lords."

"I'll risk it—if Xzan will also."

"An empty threat's no risk." Xzan was strong with contempt. "I'll treble the stake—no, raise it tenfold."

"A hundredfold?" queried Oontara.

"Done! Come on, painted warrior! Show our vacillating star king how empty the words of his champions are."

Bogaert glanced at Rounding. The Commissioner nodded almost imperceptibly. With one finger, the Colonel moved a small blue token one square.

Xzan's first expression of jubilation faded as he attempted to complete his play. Whichever way he turned, his losses mounted exponentially. His greatest strengths became his overwhelming liabilities. Even the structure of numbers seemed to join in a conspiracy against him. Finally, he had to admit a defeat more crushing than any he had ever before suffered on the gaming board. He turned to Bogaert, and there was a new line of speculation across his evil brow.

"Only once in a million games could such a sequence happen. You, Colonel Bogey, were incredibly lucky."

"I'll not deny it. But had that piece of luck not been available, I'd never have played."

"He's telling you, in his devious Terran way," interjected Oontara, "that there's absolutely no route by which he could have lost. It's the new logic, Xzan. You don't see it coming. Before you can find out what's happening, you're presented with an accomplished fact. That's how I know federation's inevitable."

"I'm glad you mentioned that," said Rounding. "It explains the purpose of our visit. Knowing my Lord Xzan was visiting, we came to make a preliminary approach regarding the advantages of membership in the Galactic Federation."

"My answer's plain," said Xzan. "You appear to have softened Oontara's skull, but you'll find me a tougher proposition. Small though my star holdings are, I still control twelve times the number of planets in your entire Federation. You're the flea that clings to the hairs of my ferocious animal. Don't bite too deeply, else my claws'll scratch you out."

"Well spoken!" said Rounding with warm approval. "But you've missed the point. A colonized planet subject to star rule has a support potential of less than one ten-thousandth of that of a self-determined, federated planet. A star colony has no incentive for self-development, since this only invites further tithes and plunder. When you consider how Terra, unaided and alone, came to join you lords and kings among the stars, you'll see how much can be achieved by the right philosophy."

"And what about the divine right of being stronger? This built star empires beyond your wildest dreams."

"I don't dream of empires, Lord Xzan. I have enough trouble just running my own department. Come, Bogey, we've taken up too much of the Lords' time. But I hope we've left Lord Xzan something to think about."

TWO

The Field of Perfection on Meon was a broad tract of rare, lush grasses maintained in such flawless condition that the name could never be doubted. Heading the slope, the impenetrable purple mountains stretched, so the legend had it, continuously up to support the arched back of the sky. Flanking the field, the walls and block towers of the twin fortress towns Andor and Ute formed a natural continuation of the mountain barrier and drew together at the foot of the slope where stood the great palace of Kam Kanizar, the King of Kings, the greatest star monarch of them all.

The children playing in the field were aware of the great tensions which beset their home world. Arma, nine Earth years old, rocked her playthings in a little cradle, and sang them an ancient hymn, as her mother might do to ease the stress. Zim was a few years older. He had a long-knife and a gimbal bow, and stalked imaginary goblins and won imaginary battles against overwhelming odds. One day he would follow his father, the mighty Kanizar, to fight the demons who dwelled among the stars; for the moment, however, not really understanding the situation, he was excited by the promise of change. The whole routine of the palace had been disturbed. Although they should have been at lessons, the children had today been awarded an unofficial holiday. Even their personal guards stood clustered in despondent discussion.

It was nearly dark before the young ones' mother, Miram, the Empress Kanizar, came to the field to fetch them. This in itself was unusual, because normally armed guardsmen would have been at her side—but this evening she came alone, as if the occasion were too personal to permit the presence of others. Tall and slender, seemingly fragile as a reed, with honey-gray hair and an air of eternal calm, she bent only slightly as she answered her children's questions.

"We mustn't be afraid, little ones. We've to be strong. Camin Sher, who pretends to your father's throne, sends many ships toward Meon. We think he means to attack us. Messengers have gone to your father, but even if he knew at this moment, he couldn't be back in time to save us."

"Then we must fight Sher ourselves."

"It isn't as easy as that, Zim. Your father has the main and both auxiliary fleets with him. We have nothing but a dozen patrol craft of the home fleet and a few supply ships. That's nowhere near enough to withstand Sher's battle fleet."

"What will we do then, Mother?"

"The Council is meeting now. Old Sashu will advise us. We think Sher's not much concerned with our garrison or installations, but that he'd like to harm you, my children. While you live, there's no substance to his Pretender's claim. Therefore, it's your safety the Council will consider most important. Whatever they say we must do without question. For your father's sake as well as your own."

She turned and led the way back across the flawless turf, with Arma holding her hand. Zim followed regretfully. Something about his mother's attitude suggested that he might never again have the chance to play under the purple mountains. Yet there was also the excitement of promised change, a break from his cloistered life. Not for one moment did he imagine that old Sashu would fail to find them safe harbor. After all, old Sashu advised Kanizar himself, and was not Kanizar the king of all the kings?

Leaving her children in the care of a trusted retainer, Miram returned to her chambers and spent some time examining her treasures, mainly gifts Kam Kanizar had brought her from the most exotic places in the galaxy. She knew that with the coming of Camin Sher these things must pass from her possession. Such loss would fill her with regret, but it was a pain which could be tolerated. Her children, however, were different. No matter what the hardship or personal cost, they must be brought to safety. This was not only political expediency, but also a necessity of the heart. Night enveloped her as she sat and made her silent dedication.

A whisper of drapes heralded the arrival of old Sashu, who was older and more wise in the affairs of the galaxy and of men than anyone else Miram had ever met. His creased and wizened face held a sympathetic understanding of her mood, yet his eyes were steady with his customary resolve.

"Is the Council decided?" asked Miram. Her voice sounded tired, reflecting the strains of the day.

"I've decided, my Lady, and the Council doesn't disagree. For the safety of yourself and the Kanizar line, you and the children must leave Meon within the hour. You'll travel incognito on a freighter already charted for Ortel. To cover your departure, our entire fleet, such as it is, will mount an attack on Sher's war fleet. The Pretender will certainly win, but it should buy us the time we need to get the freighter out unobserved."

Miram considered the prospect and its consequences. She felt numb.

"Such loss of life. Is there no other way?"

"My Lady"—Sashu's voice was infinitely soft—"every man in the fleet was born for this moment. Though it means certain death, there'll not be one dissenter. Further discussion is useless. We've none of us any choice."

"Forgive me, Sashu. I wasn't questioning your judgment, only regretting a terrible waste. When we reach Ortel, do we throw ourselves on the mercy of Oontara?"

"I fear not, my Lady. Since Oontara's infatuation with the Federation, his whole court has become riddled with spies. Rumor has it that Lord Xzan even now is his guest, and we know how Xzan favors the Pretender. No, you must remain incognito and strive to contact Manu Kan. He's a worthy kinsman of ours, and a merchant of considerable influence in Tenarensor. He's Kanizar's man, and he'll guard you well. Entreat him to smuggle you to Terra, where you'll be safe. Not even the Pretender would dare raise a finger against those 'terrible infants' of the galaxy."

"But why should the Terrans protect us? They've no treaty with Kanizar."

"It's what's known as the new logic. They'll protect you not because you bring Kanizar's heirs, but because you're a mother in distress."

She nodded dully, not relishing the idea of the days ahead. "What retinue is coming with me?"

"None, my Lady. It's safer for the three of you to travel alone. Guards and attendants can't fail to attract attention, and Tenarensor has more spies than inhabitants. You'll carry no jewels or treasures. You'll be dressed in very simple clothes. Even your beauty will be a danger to you. Once off the ship, you must wear a widow's cowl at all times. Do you understand?"

"I hear you, faithful Sashu. I'll take your advice, just as my Lord Kanizar has always done. My regret is that you'll not be there to share the safety we attain."

"Have no concern for old Sashu. It is you who carry the burden. Prince Zim is the most valuable child in the galaxy. With respect, my Lady, you've known little of life outside the courts and palaces of kings. Thus, the journey will fall infinitely harder on you than it would on a serving woman. If I didn't know your inner strengths, I'd be mortally afraid. As it is, I've complete confidence that the heirs of Kanizar are in safe hands."

"You say we leave within the hour?"

"The freighter's already waiting on the pads. We wait only to get the home fleet into space on the light side. Then the freighter will make space from the dark side, keeping Meon between the ship and the Pretender's fleet. With luck, the freighter will be out of scanner range before Sher has disposed of the trickle of ships we send to meet him. It could be many days before he even knows you're gone."

"May the gods bless you, Sashu, and see you safe through the coming darkness."

"And may the darkness hide you, Miram, till you come to the safety of Terra's light. Come, it's time you made ready! My ears tell me the home fleet is ready for launch. We come to the most terrible night in creation."

On the bridge of his flagship, Camin Sher, the Pretender, watched the screens with interest and mounting jubilation. Against the might of the war fleet at his back the defenders of Meon were offering only token resistance: twelve small patrol vessels. Kanizar's second auxiliary fleet, which Sher had feared to meet, was mercifully as absent as his agents had suggested it would be. It was a major tactical blunder on the part of Kanizar, and one which the Pretender was determined the King of Kings would always regret. The rich lands of Meon were open for rape, and the palace was ready for plunder. More important, the stock of Kanizar's bloodline could be destroyed in public view, leaving no other claimants to the throne once Kanizar himself was dead.

One of his spacefinders blossomed suddenly, and the glare brought Sher back from speculation to the immediate tactics of battle. The spacefinder had been vaporized, its position now marked only by a broad streak of ion-contaminated debris. The cause of this disaster was not immediately apparent, until Sher thought to count the Meon ships. Eleven. Suddenly Sher realized he had underestimated the defense. This handful of ships set against him was not going to engage in conventional battle. They were on a suicide mission.

Each would select a target ship, match coordinates precisely, then leap straight into hyperdrive. From a position well out of weapons range, they would streak at megalight velocities as if to pass through the target vessel. There was no defense against such a maneuver, and the results were inevitable: the complete destruction of both vessels. It was tactical brilliance for a defense which was bound to be beaten. For Camin Sher, it meant insupportably high losses.

While he pondered the problem, two of his major destroyers, each with a complement of better than two thousand men, became red roses and ceased to register as anything more substantial than gas. Since the attacking patrol ships had a probable crew of, at most, only four men, the ratio of his losses was at least five hundred to one, and nothing in his fleet was sacred, no matter how perfect its armor.

It took Sher two further agonized seconds to realize that his own flagship would be a prime objective. As he ordered emergency lifecraft evacuation, he was sick with the thought that he might already have delayed too long. Like a shoal of startled fish darting from a whale, the lifecraft departed, mere moments before the flagship became a miniature nova, which produced enough radiation to knock a couple of years off the Pretender's life expectancy. White and shaken, he lay on the life-craft's floor and waited helplessly while eight more of his finest dreadnoughts became suns. Then he knew the battle was over, and that because of numerical suprem-acy he had certainly won. However, the bitter flavor of defeat was strong in his mouth as he ordered the rem-nants of his once-great battle fleet to begin the sack of Meon.

Meanwhile, on the night side of the planet, a freighter slipped ponderously into hyperdrive and sped away across the great vortex of the Milky Way, heading for Ortel.

THREE

The gaming continued far into the night, with the players so evenly matched that neither could gain a de-cisive advantage. In an attempt to raise the interest, the stakes were growing ever higher. The ownership of star systems rested on the turn of a token. Although there were some considerable runs, nothing occurred to equal the remarkable performance of Colonel Bogaert, and the players were becoming bored through lack of excite-ment.

"Old friend," said Oontara after a while, "I never thought to admit it, but the war game no longer moves me. It has battles without blood, victories without the screams of the defeated, and defeats without bitter an-ger waking the will to survive."

"I was thinking on the same lines," said Xzan. "These token warriors remind me of your Terran friends. Somebody paints a value on them, and that's the unit they become—without earning their place by blood and fire."

"I agree about the tokens, but not about the Terrans. You misjudge them simply because they don't conform to our standards. But they're a race new to the stars—why should they bother to conform? I once went into battle against them, and found myself completely outclassed. I tell you, they're unassailable."

"As a race, possibly." Xzan lacked conviction. "As individuals, they're pale, flat apologies for fighting men. In my retinue right now I've one I'd dare set against any ten Terrans and back him with my life—providing the Terrans fought man to man and not with the forces of their technology."

"A useless proviso. You can't separate Terrans from their technology. Take it away from them and they recreate it. Never commit your life to such a gamble. You'd all too easily find the odds reversed against you."

"If you think so, you've never seen my champion." Xzan reached for the golden tassel and summoned a servant. "Have my Captain send Bethschant immediately. I wish to show King Oontara what the complete fighting man looks like."

The servant returned shortly with a soldier in the uniform of Xzan's personal guard. Oontara regarded the appointee with mixed surprise and fascination. Here stood not one of Xzan's vaunted hereditary warriors, but a near-animal creature, with a squat, hairy body and overlong arms which rippled with an abundance of muscle. His face was flat, fleshy, and fully as wicked as his master's. Scarcely a centimeter of skin on his face and body did not bear the scar of some past wound or disease, yet his stance and bearing were of one driven by a life force which acknowledged death as the only true conqueror.

"This is your champion?" Oontara's voice was strong with disbelief.

"You'll find no better. He's a very clever devil, is Bethschant. His guile and lack of conscience give no limit to his talent for mixing with death and surviving the consequences. We speak of hereditary warriors, but here's one to end them all—a hereditary survivor."

"Is he from a star world?"

"No. From Avida—where the life pressures are so extreme that ninety-five percent of the population never reach puberty. Only the successful scion of successful scion ever manage to breed. A hundred thousand years of this has produced a race of the most indestructible individuals the galaxy's ever seen."

"And the ugliest," said Oontara with a shudder. "I didn't know Avida had a human population."

"It hasn't now. The total colony was less than a hundred strong. When the system came under my control, I took them all into my service. They make magnificent warriors—even the women. Show me the Terran who could survive a week on Avida, much less grow to maturity there."

"You persistently miss the point. Terrans don't adapt to foreign environments. They use their technology to adapt the environment to them. A Terran colony on Avida would remain Terran—it's the planet which would have to change."

"I can see how this might apply to colonies—but we're discussing individuals. You can't seriously think an isolated Terran could survive on Avida?"

"The question's one of degree. The more Terrans you have, the more technology they generate. How much needs to be generated to insure the survival of a man? They've a saying: 'What can't be endured must be cured.' It's the philosophy which makes these terrible children so terrible."

Xzan dismissed Bethschant with a nod of his head and turned back conspiratorially to the star king.

"Our differences won't be resolved by argument. You're a gambler, Oontara. Would you dare put your viewpoint to the test?"

"If you've a fair proposal."

"I suggest we each put a champion on Avida for a set period. One shall be Bethschant, the other a Terran of your choice. The game's to see which can survive for the agreed term."

"I said a fair proposal," said Oontara. "We already know Bethschant can survive on Avida. The point under discussion is whether my candidate could do the same. Furthermore, if a Terran's to survive he must have a nucleus of bits of wire and things with which to practice his technology. To do otherwise would be equivalent to putting Bethschant there with his arms cut off."

"I accept your second point with reservations. The first I'll not give. Bethschant survived on Avida because he belonged to a colony. This time he'll be alone. So whoever's candidate survives shall be the winner. If neither or both survive, the game's void."

"Not so fast!" Oontara was fully equal to his wily opponent. "If neither survives, it establishes nothing except that the game was too severe. If both survive, it proves my Terran the equal of your savage, therefore the game's mine."

"You drive a hard bargain, friend. I see the soft life's little dimmed your cunning. I concede the point—but only if the odds make the gaming worth my while."

"What wager had you in mind?"

"Would you risk ownership of fifty habitable planets against ten of mine? Such an acquisition could make me a king the equal of yourself."

"I'm faintly interested, though I've not said I agree."

"Come! Where's the old Oontara, who'd risk all on the placing of a token? Have you really grown soft, as I feared? Or do you have sudden doubts about the omnipotence of Terra?"

"Your jibes are misplaced, Xzan. It's not that I thought the stakes too high, but rather that they were low. The wager still lacks interest. Ten of your miserable, gutted mudballs seems little enough recompense for the proof of my point. I'll offer a new condition, binding on us both. I doubt you've sufficient faith even to consider it."

"I'd dare anything to teach you the lesson you deserve."

"Then here's what I propose. I'll wager fifty planets against your ten, as proof of my certainty. My further commitment's that, if I lose, I'll renounce my contracts with Terra and return to the old ways—if, in the event of my winning, you'll agree to surrender all your holdings to the Federation."

"If I didn't know you for a joker, I'd think you serious."

"I'm perfectly serious, Xzan. It's you who finds the challenge difficult to face. Who's the softer of us now?"

"You raise the bid to a desperate level. But somebody has to show you the error of your ways. The chances to take fifty of your planets and also bring you back to sanity is too good to miss. I accept your condition, Oontara. I've named my champion. Let's hear the name of yours."

"There are many I might choose. But we were speaking of Terrans in the abstract. Therefore, I'll pick one I've only just met. I nominate Colonel Bogey."

A smile of wicked anticipation lit Xzan's face. "An interesting choice—though I doubt if Commissioner Rounding will happily volunteer his services."

"The fat Commissioner doesn't need to know. In past days, Xzan, we manipulated many and much by stealth and cunning. Well, I've not forgotten the old tricks. If you'll guarantee to deliver your champion to Avida, I'll guarantee the delivery of mine. But we've not yet agreed on the matter of equipment and provisions. What do you say for Bethschant?"

"He's a nomad and a hunter. Too many provisions would be a burden. I think such spears and native weapons as he had when I acquired him, plus a long-knife, and prepared food for no more than three days. That will insure his rapid return to the old ways of living."

"And I see for Colonel Bogey perhaps the basic stores and tool pack which are given to a star-world settler joining a colony."

"Since there'll be no colony for him to join, I can scarcely make objection. Though what use he'll find for hammering nails and digging trenches on Avida is beyond my comprehension."

"Then it's settled! All we need to establish is the duration of the game."

"I've been thinking about that. Would three months be too severe?"

"Let's make it six, to be decisive. And, Xzan . . ."

"Yes?"

"This time, let there be no interference with the fortunes of the game—else the prize goes to the other party by default."

"Naturally! Then we're agreed, Oontara. Though I can't seriously believe you think you can win. It'll be pleasant enough to welcome you back to the ways of your fathers. If age hasn't tried you too sorely, you'll likely find a few more planets to replace those you'll have lost."

"You count too soon, Xzan. It's your way of life on trial here. And you who'll have to make the reparations. I've told you, federation is inevitable. I speak from strength of knowledge. I merely go a little from my way to help an old friend who's become too blind to see the path ahead."

FOUR

A freighter carved its way out of parking orbit into Ortel's ruby night and dropped with the sound of a million demons onto the landing pads of Tenarensor spaceport. A heavy cargo vessel, she was routed to the extreme edge of the field, well away from the passenger-receiving docks.

Old Sashu had made the preparations well, and the liberal bribes bestowed on Meon were being honored fully. A woman wearing a widow's cowl was silently hustled through the warehouses and across the perimeter hardstand. She was followed by two hushed, intensely excited children. The trio was led finally through a small metal gate and onto a street bordering the bewildering commercial district which lay beyond. At this point, all obligations had been met. Shorn suddenly of even hired support, the woman drew her children against the comforting folds of her cloak and looked about uncertainly, not sure of what move to make next.

In the dim maroon of night, the bustle of spaceport trade continued unabated; space schedules heeded no local light or darkness. Somewhere among the moving bulks of floats and transporters there ought to be a guide to meet her—somebody to take them to a place of rest and temporary safety. Tenarensor, however, was a very large place, and there was no certainty they were even at the right exit from the spaceport. Miram had a map and emergency directions, but these would be of little use before the coming of daylight. Nor could they reasonably remain in the vicinity of the delivery gate without attracting attention. Without a real objective in mind, she picked up the few poor bags which contained their meager belongings and began to walk slowly along the road, telling the children to keep their faces shaded from the street flares to avoid any possibility of recognition.

After half a kilometer, she had an uneasy feeling that someone was following them. A quiet shadow, dark against the shades of the red night, sought shelter whenever she looked behind. Though she could not have sworn it was always the same person, the behavior was repeated too often to be ignored. So conscious did she become of the lurking presence that she nearly missed the significance of a few short notes of music whistled casually by a man inspecting boxes on a float. Only on the second hearing did her mind acknowledge the theme of Kanizar's favorite battle hymn.

"Lady Miram!" The float was almost completely blocking the road behind them.

"Yes. You come from Manu Kan?"

"Indeed. But this is no place for idle talk. The Pretender's spies had rumor of your coming. They're all around the area. All of you on the float—quickly!"

Miram helped the children climb aboard, then seized the thick hand that reached down to assist her. At first sight, the piled boxes offered only a precarious handhold. Then she realized that the boxes were piled to form thick walls, with a hollow cavity within. Inside, a rough cabin had been constructed to bear the weight of the boxes stacked above. The guide led them into the cabin and replaced the boxes which formed the entrance.

"Welcome to Ortel, my Lady! Sorry about the conveyance, but the Pretender's men are everywhere. Fortunately, they can't yet be certain you've arrived. We'll try to spirit you away before they're sure. The price on your heads would make a thousand men wealthy, so they won't hesitate to attack if they find out where you are."

"Someone followed us along the road from the spaceport gate."

"Hmm!" The guide checked the ion gun at his waist and leaned forward between the boxes to speak to the driver. Then he moved a single box and wriggled through, replacing it from outside. Miram and the children waited in the darkness, aware of the swaying of the slowly moving float. Then came the abrupt, miniature thunder characteristic of an ion-weapon discharge. Soon the boxes at the door were removed, and their guide reentered.

"May the gods give us speed! Now they've no witnesses to your arrival. But when they find three of their own men dead, they'll know just as surely you were here."

"Where're you taking us?"

"To one of Manu Kan's private places. There you'll be safe till we can get you passage to Terra. But we've a good distance to cover yet."

The implications of the last sentence were underscored when the float stopped suddenly. They heard the sound of argument. The guide crept to the hole through which he communicated with the driver and listened.

"Ortellian Guards. They know something's afoot, but they're not sure what. They're operating a random stop-and-search pattern."

"Will they find us here?"

"Only by chance. Manu has nearly a hundred floats like this on the road tonight. It would be impossible to search them all, especially since they're loaded with lead pellets."

"What would happen if they did discover us?"

"It would be wise to admit who you were. You'd be taken to King Oontara, who'd probably offer you his protection. Unfortunately, his court crawls with spies and assassins. There's no real safety for you there."

After a few moments, the float again proceeded on its way. The driver called back something through the hole, and the guide relayed the information.

"The guards were satisfied, but the Pretender's agents weren't. They've already attacked one of Manu's floats about a kilometer ahead and killed the driver. If I know Manu, he'll use the excuse to turn all hell abroad in Tenarensor tonight."

"Does that mean much fighting?"

"Aye, my Lady. That's why the guards are jumpy. With the value of Manu's cargoes so high, he's well versed in the arts of protection. He'll treat this as a commercial war."

"Which it isn't."

"No, but it'll confuse the issue sufficiently to give us a chance of getting through."

For ten minutes the float continued on its way without obstruction. Then its progress was suddenly arrested by a violent shock, which threw them all to the floor. Regaining his feet, the guide went to consult with the driver. When he turned back, his voice was grave.

"An ambush, Lady Miram. Strings of floats across the road. We're going to try to ram a passage through. If we can't, we'll have to fight. No matter what happens, don't try to leave. Stay on the floor and protect your heads from concussion if you can."

"I understand. May the gods guard your progress!"

With a swift reassembly of the boxes which hid the door, the guide left the cabin. Miram brought her children together, and they sat on the littered floor while she distributed clothing from her bags to protect their heads with. This action was taken not a moment too soon. The float was again urged into motion and then brought to a halt with a cruel shock. Again and again it staggered into battle, and each time was deflected sideways, to scrape hideously along some forbidding mass until halted by forces greater than its own very considerable momentum.

Then came the noise of shooting. It started nearby, and advanced and retreated many times, with only fancy to suggest the fortunes of the combatants. The whipcrack thunder of ion weapons echoed spitefully from walls and buildings; occasionally the sound was nearly continuous. Miram found it peculiarly terrifying not to be able to see the progress of the fight or know if her champions were holding their ground or being beaten. With a sick heart, she imagined that they were losing, and that by the intensity of their effort they had betrayed the fact that they had something important to defend. She cradled young Zim's shoulders with her arms and bade him to be brave.

To her surprise, he shrugged her away. He had imagined the fortunes of the battle quite differently, and was softly cheering victory. In this he displayed his father's optimism and love of combat. Had it been permitted, he would certainly have been happier to have joined the fighting, instead of being forced to sit in the darkness listening to it rage around him. Miram caught his sense of helplessness and frustration at being confined, and knew it was only in deference to her wishes that he remained. She understood that one day soon even her influence would be unable to tame the Kanizar blood, and that he too would blaze a destructive trail across the galaxy, as had his father.

There was a deafening explosion close by. The float gave a sickening lurch and settled roughly to the ground as its motors died. Then came the sound of many running feet, and the sudden entrance of red light as the stack of boxes blocking the door was toppled off the float, leaving the entrance bare.

"I thought as much!"

A huge figure, pistol in hand, thrust through the opening and stood trying to adjust his eyes to the darkness of the cabin. Arma whimpered with fright, and the pistol turned in her direction. Immediately Zim was off the floor, the wrap which his mother had given him thrown straight in the intruder's face. The gun arm went up as the startled man attempted to protect his face from he knew not what. Zim came up under his elbow and forced the arm yet higher. The gun went off.

The whipcrack of the discharge in the confined space deafened them all, and the blaze of energy went straight up into the boxes piled above the cabin, creating a fire-flash so intense that its image interfered with Miram's sight for a long period afterward. The miraculous thing was the reaction of their would-be assailant. For half a second he reeled in the doorway; then, with a blood-chilling yell, he leaped backward, falling to the roadbed from the superstructure of the float, dropped his weapon, and ran off uttering hoarse and anguished moans. He had covered scarcely ten meters before a bolt dropped him in mid-stride.

Miram was not certain whether to cry with relief or be sick. Zim, unharmed, was staring with great surprise at the doorway through which the vanquished assassin had departed. The overwhelming stench of burned flesh told its own peculiar story. The assassin had fired his weapon directly upward—and the energy of the dis-charge had penetrated the boxes above, liquefying some of the lead pellets they contained. Their assailant had bathed his own head with molten lead—a fitting if un-premeditated justice for the assault on the heirs of Kani-zar.

Their guide came running back to them, his face a cloud of concern.

"Lady Miram—thank the gods you're safe! That devil slipped through our net. What a mercy he didn't attack!"

"He did," said Miram, her calmness returning. "For-tunately, I had my own protector."

The puzzled frown on the guide's face deepened when he went to examine the body of the fallen assas-sin. He returned full of speculation, looking first at the ruptured boxes and then at Zim. Then, gravely, he un-buckled the weapon belt from his own waist and placed it around the boy. Astonished, Zim hesitated, then took the heavy weapon from its holster and tested the grip with his hand. It was a perfect fit.

The young prince looked at his mother as though despairingly asking permission to keep so dangerous yet marvelous a gift. Miram stifled her horrified reaction. This was a situation to which she had long since reconciled herself.

"If you've really finished with childhood so soon, accept it proudly, Zim. For what you've done today I think your father would have offered you his own."

The guide gave the boy a respectful salute. "Hail, chip off Kanizar!" he said genially. "Manu Kan will be preparing an account of this night's work. I think the King of Kings will be pleased to know his seed breeds true."

FIVE

Hilary Rounding had a whole suite of offices in the superb new buildings of the Terran Outspace Technical Aid Commission. He was seldom to be found there, however. More usually he was wandering the great ornamental corridors of Oontara's court, talking to nobles and minor star lords and listening to the gossip and scandals of the star community. In such a way, he kept a sure finger on the pulse of the Hub worlds, using Oontara's court as a barometer for measuring the strengths and moods of the star factions.

For ten days now the rumor had persisted that Miram, the Empress Kanizar, had fled to Ortel from Meon to escape the forces of the Pretender. Rounding tended to dismiss the idea. What could she gain by fleeing to Ortel, when she could reach some more neutral dynasty without crossing the vortex of the Hub? The only advantage Ortel had to offer was its position along the route of the Federation starliners, whose ultimate destination was Terra. Since Kam Kanizar frequently spoke contemptuously of the Federation, it appeared unlikely that Miram would be en route to Terra. There was also the fact that, although Miram was thought to have landed in Tenarensor, nobody had the slightest idea of what had happened to her thereafter.

Another rumor—one not so widespread, but far more disturbing—ran that Oontara and his guest Xzan had fallen out over the former's dalliance with the Federation. To settle the dispute, a survival game had been arranged, in which two champions, one of whom was to be a Terran, would be placed in some hostile environment to determine which of them was better suited to survive. Oontara was openly criticized for accepting a huge wager when he had a full knowledge of Xzan's capacity for cheating.

This second rumor Rounding took seriously. Although Oontara professed genuine leanings toward federation, he was still a star savage by tradition and inclination. The notion of a survival game fitted convincingly with what Rounding knew of the star king's humor and his disregard for life. About Xzan the Commissioner could have believed anything. That star lord's notorious love of gaming had caused whole planetary populations to be murdered to satisfy some whim of chance, and his capacity for cruelty was a legend.

With the idea of a survival game a virtual certainty, Rounding's immediate concern was over which Terran had been selected as the victim. One absolute certainty was that the game could not be allowed to take place with a Terran participant. First, there was the moral issue of Terra's responsibility toward her employees who worked outspace. Second, the idea that Terrans could be used as pawns in alien star games was a notion to be swiftly discouraged.

The Commissioner's inquiries around the courtrooms on this particular morning had a more than usually searching quality. The rumor had originated within the court of Oontara. This lent credence to its probability, but made it less understandable how the star king could have allowed the story to circulate where he must have known the Terran Commissioner must hear of it. Learning nothing to his satisfaction, Rounding sought an audience with Oontara, determined to set the matter straight.

Unusually, he was admitted to see the star monarch immediately. Oontara sat at his great desk of state, sorting through documents, and seemed glad of the opportunity to talk.

"My dear Commissioner, sit and take wine. Do you know the main consequence of negotiation with Terra? It's an exponential increase in the paperwork."

"I've long suspected it, my Lord. But it's about personnel rather than paperwork that I came to see you."

"Indeed? You've the look of a man with a problem on his mind. Come, my federated friend. According to the new logic, your problems are mine also."

Rounding made his reply a tactful accusation, and finished with a few veiled threats of what might occur if the survival game became a reality. Oontara listened with increasing noises of distress, which were not supported by the wicked lines at the sides of his eyes.

"My dear Rounding! I'd thought we'd grown to understand each other better."

"I'm sure we do understand each other, my Lord. That's why I hastened to you for reassurance there's no truth in the rumor."

"You did rightly. Such wild talk can only make mischief between us. You've my most categorical denial that any such scheme ever entered my head. However, it's a fortunate meeting, Commissioner. I've a favor to ask.'"

"If it's within my power, it's yours."

"I believe you're interested in the *ransad*."

"Very much so! And a fascinating topic it is, too. A developing technology which reached unprecedented heights—then mysteriously ceased to develop further. Did you know they preceded Terra by as much as a million years in developing space flight and the hyperdrive? And its originators have vanished entirely, leaving their technology scattered around the galaxy, to become petrified into custom and ritual."

"All you say is true, Commissioner—though we of the stars have always thought of it as *the* knowledge. To us it had no beginning and no end. It was a singularity and a totality, incapable of being improved. It gained a new perspective when you showed us that Terran technology is unending. Therefore, as a cultural exercise, I'd like to finance one of your Terran experts to do some practical research into the *ransad*. Such as where it began, why it ceased to progress, and what befell its originators."

"I'd be happy to arrange that for you. Did you have anyone particular in mind?"

"The one you call Colonel Bogey. He impressed me greatly."

"Research isn't strictly Bogey's line."

"I was emphasizing the practical nature of the project. This could well include exploratory trips to possible star locations. It would need a man of his caliber."

"I'll see what can be arranged," said Rounding speculatively. "But he's on loan to me from the Space Service. You may have to wait till I get a replacement out from Terra."

"Do your best, Commissioner. Both Lord Xzan and I were greatly impressed by his immediate grasp of a complex problem. I see him as an outstanding man who needs the chance to prove himself."

"In Terran terms, the Colonel's already proved himself, or he'd not be out here. But I'm sure he'd welcome the extra scope. I'll talk to him and see if he can be persuaded."

"Thank you, Commissioner. You see, we do have mutual understanding."

"But why me?" asked Bogaert angrily. "I've worked years to qualify for this posting. Now you want to smuggle me back to Terra like a small boy in disgrace."

"You're reading it all wrong. I know these star savages. They've a penchant for playing games with human lives. I can't allow you to take such a risk for their amusement or to satisfy a wager."

"Fine! Most of my work can be done within the Commission complex. Surely I don't need retreat to Terra?"

"You're making two errors, Bogey, old son. You're underestimating that wicked old bastard Oontara and just how much he can manipulate the scene. If he wants you in a game, then you're in it no matter what you think. You also missed the point that once it becomes established that Terrans are good pawns for gaming, the sport could become a galactic pastime. Do you fancy being the first of a succession of human fighting cocks?"

"Of course not, but—"

"There aren't any buts. We're a small race in a big galaxy where the life of an individual counts for nothing. But it's our standards which've got to succeed, because we're cursed with being unique. So far as we know, every other race in the galaxy is dependent on the *ransad* for its technology. We didn't have the *ransad*. We brought ourselves into space by scientific method and a bloody-minded refusal to be daunted by the impossible. Now we've arrived, and we've got something to sell in both hardware and philosophy. Nothing and nobody's going to reduce Terra to the status of an ordinary star world and a plaything for star kings."

"I don't see that that's in question," said Bogaert.

"Oontara and Xzan are questioning it. So we have two courses of action. We can play you against a stacked deck and, win or lose, establish Terrans as good material for games. Or we can treat the whole thing with contempt and get you out of the path of their temptation."

"What makes you say the deck's stacked?"

"It's never otherwise on the Hub. Fair play's a peculiar Terran concept. Oontara led us into this—and he's supposed to be our friend. So just think how that Satan's limb Xzan views the prospect. He's fighting for recognition as a star king. He wouldn't give a damn if a thousand million died to achieve his end."

Bogaert shook his head ruefully. "You've made your point, Hilary. When do I leave?"

"As soon as can be arranged—perhaps a couple of days. We don't dare divert a starliner here, because it would attract too much attention. I'll arrange for you to be smuggled out on a space barge to make rendezvous with the next Terra-bound liner which hits this sector. And, Bogey . . ."

"Yes?"

"Don't take all this as any reflection on yourself. I'd personally back you in a survival game against anyone Xzan could muster. Unfortunately, the politics of the situation don't allow us to compete."

Bogaert looked at his nails and grinned reflectively. "I used to wonder how a fat, short-assed politician ever got to be Commissioner in a theater like the Hub. Now I know. The only way you can beat a star savage is to pit against him someone even more primitive and potentially more savage than he is."

"If you've learned that much, your time on the Hub hasn't been wasted."

"Still, it's a damn shame about the *ransad*. I'd have loved to have taken Oontara at face value and had a crack at the problem."

"And I. There are many curious parallels between the *ransad* and Terran science. In some areas, they're virtually interchangeable. Take the present mysticism away from the *ransad* and you find a system of reasoned knowledge far greater than our own. In contrast, Terran science seems hasty and utilitarian. We never had the time to probe too deeply into areas of knowledge for which we had no immediate practical application. So there are still huge portions of the *ransad* we can't even begin to understand."

"And no clues about its originators?"

"Only inferences. They were weaker in atomic physics than is Terran science, but leagues ahead in relativity. This suggests they weren't pressured by their environment to develop the crude power devices which kicked Terra into the main atomic phase. And it's a certainty that their intellectual powers were well above the galactic norm. Their optical instruments peak in the Terran visual range, from which we infer that in eye structure, at least, they were very like ourselves and probably evolved under similar conditions. In fact, many aspects of the *ransad's* originators seem less alien to us than do the races who enjoy its use."

"No clues even about where it developed?"

"None. It could have been anywhere in the galaxy, or even out of it. I suspect it was within this galaxy, for the very simple reason that the *ransad's* conclusions have been doctored."

"Doctored?"

"Those like the star kings, who use the *ransad* for their technology, swear that it's the ultimate in knowledge and can't be exceeded. We know this is nonsense. But there's evidence that the higher *ransad* texts have been deliberately tailored to give that impression. The compilers of the *ransad* didn't want something to be known."

"Do we have any idea what that something was?"

"At a guess, it was intergalactic drive systems. The *ransad* states they're an all-time impossibility. Yet Terra has one on active test right now. With their vast lead in relativity studies, the originators of the *ransad* must've known that intergalactic drives are theoretically at least as viable as conventional hyperdrives. That suggests to me that the *ransad* technologists evolved in our own galaxy but left to populate another—after making damn sure the warring star kings couldn't follow."

"Which shows they were also people of discernment and good sense," said Bogaert sourly. "Having met Oontara and Xzan, I have a desire to make a similar move myself. I can understand the *ransad's* originators' going, but I don't understand what they gained by leaving so much powerful technology behind them."

"I don't suppose we'll ever know their motives, though one likes to believe they were similar to our own. But here's a point to think about. Spread right across the Terran civilizations existing around two thousand and sixteen hundred B.C. there's a sudden emphasis on the development of writing, of systems of government, and working in bronze. Wouldn't you know it, but that's exactly the territory of the first book of *ransad* texts. Did we actually get Book One on Terra all those years ago? And, if so, what reason had they for not trusting us with Book Two?"

SIX

Dropping out of hyperspace, the wicked-looking ship of Xzan's personal command force made a swift orbit around Avida. The proficiency of the black vessel in executing this maneuver betrayed its long familiarity in gaining orbital battle stations around neutral worlds destined to be afflicted by the star lord's craving for dominance.

This time, however, no terrifying missiles were unleashed. Only one lifecraft descended from the vicious father ship, and this delivered to the surface not a destructive squadron but a solitary individual. The weapons which were laid on the soil were not war floats or projectile carriers, but only such things as a man might carry: a spear, a blowpipe, a throwing stick, flints, a bow, some stores, and a long-knife. The individual savored the air, checked his supplies, gathered his belongings into manageable bundles, and set off into the forest fringes without a backward glance, as if escape from the service of Xzan was something greatly welcomed.

Curiously, Xzan had kept his promise. The weapons and supplies with which Bethschant had been provided were only those few simple things which had been agreed to by Oontara. Only one thing had been added outside the scope of the arrangement, and that was the command given to Bethschant: "If Avida doesn't kill Colonel Bogey, then finish the job yourself."

The instruction was no burden for the wily savage. Avida was his birthplace. He knew it as a relentless enemy. With full knowledge of the dangers and pitfalls, he still had fears for his own survival, having been off-planet in the service of Xzan for five Avidan years. Such absence had dulled the lifetime habit of never relaxing for an instant against the constant dangers. He would need all of his exceptional sight and hearing and talent for survival just to stay alive. What chance, then, had a soft and inexperienced Terran of surviving even a few days in such a place?

Realizing the need to reacclimate himself, Bethschant had opted to be placed on Avida well before the Colonel was due to arrive. He needed a period in which to adapt again to the harsh way of life. There were also differences to be overcome between the condition of his former years and his present situation. Previously he had lived with a tribal group, which always moved in unison, so that help was only a cry away. Now he was on his own. He was the only member of his species on this whole vast and savage planet. The entire remaining human population of Avida had been "liberated" into space by Xzan's probing ships, and the knowledge of this fact emphasized the silence that lay over the great forests and swamp tracts.

The demands of survival, however, were too fierce to permit him to brood on his loneliness. His first action had been to get clear of the flux-reaction range of the departing lifecraft. The next consideration was to find a place in which to spend the night, because it was already too late to make a tree camp. The old survival rituals, which he had thought he never again would need, began to flood back into memory. He deliberately chose a clearing in a thorn thicket as a likely campsite. It was only in exploring it that he realized how much he had forgotten.

He had chosen the thicket to give him protection against large predators, but a single contact with a thorn warned him that the predators might be preferable to the protection. He looked in amazement and concern as the slight puncture on his arm became a vivid blue weal, the toxins making the veins stand out beneath the skin like a web of iron. He cursed himself savagely for not having remembered that thornbush. Nature had provided him with strong immunity to Avidan poisons, but he knew it would cost him many hours of fever before his arm, rapidly growing stiff, again became usable.

It became imperative that he immediately make camp for the night. The fever was already coming upon him, and he had only one arm with which to make the preparations. With his throwing stick, he probed the ground for a suitable spot, found one near the thorn hedge, and, holding a flint between his toes, bent to the task of making fire. Such was his skill and the combustibility of Avidan firebush that he soon had a good blaze going.

When the fire was fully hot, he heaped on it as many branches and leaves as possible, then spread the flaming mass over a wide area. Having assured himself that the whole area would become properly scorched, he left the fire and cut the broad fronds he would need to make a cover. Although he was barely on the fringes of the forest, the presence of tall trees meant that he would have to protect himself while sleeping against airborne particles of acid sap.

Then, taking up a long, tubular vessel, he went to the edge of the swamp and scooped the filthy black water from the shallows. So active were the hair-fine fleshworms in the sludge that he could see them waving their wiry ends above the rim of the pot, sensing by some blind instinct the nearness of his body. Returning to his camping spot, he raked dying embers from the fire, crushed the ashes with a stone, and quenched the mess with water. In a second tubular vessel he made a crude filter with the ash, and allowed the remaining water to trickle through it before he dared drink. The sourness of the dilute lye leached from the ash made his mouth sore, but at least the water was free of fleshworms and, he hoped, other equally vicious constituents. It was a procedure every native of Avida had to learn almost before he could walk if he was to stand any chance of survival. What hope, therefore, would there be for an uninitiated Terran?

His left arm was now swollen beyond use, and the

fever brought perspiration trickling from his brow. He raked aside the remaining ashes of the fire with a stick and probed the ground beneath. The crustiness told him that the vicious shoots and flesh-seeking creatures in the soil would be deterred at least until morning. He hoped his fever would pass before the thrusting forces of nature broke through the charred ground cover and began to attack his resting body. He laid himself down on the uncomfortably hot patch of soil he had sterilized, and began to arrange the cover above him so that he would not easily disturb it in his sleep. His spear he cradled against his chest, ready for instant use. The poisonous thorn shrub would protect his back, but the growing fever left him incapable of maintaining a proper watch on the remaining unprotected sides. He therefore consigned his safe journey through till morning to the strange gods of Avida, and closed his eyes and slept.

Because of the fever and the toxins in his bloodstream, his sleep was fitful and disturbed. Perhaps Avida was reaching out to her only son, striving to reestablish the old rapport between habitat and inhabitant. Whatever the reason, his dreams returned constantly to the old way of life, to the fears and the failures, the hardships and the hatreds. It brought to mind the old legends of the days when his people were said to have controlled Avida instead of living like animals destined for extinction.

The gods, it seemed, were pleased with his devotions. Bethschant awoke the next morning slightly surprised to find himself still alive. The fever was gone and his arm nearly returned to normal. He felt considerably refreshed and confident. His first act of the day was to greet the sunshine and the heady air with one immense cry of animal exuberance, which echoed back from the startled forest and the distant mountains as if in response to his greeting. Mankind had returned to Avida, and a new challenge was being offered to old enemies.

Bethschant was back.

SEVEN

For the last ten meters he had no cover at all. Leaving the shadow of the work float, Bogaert decided to take the risk, and ran upright through the red darkness to where the outriders of the spacebarge loomed high and dark. Gaining the hull of the pod, he pressed himself against it and paused, slightly breathless, as he surveyed the field, wondering if he had been observed. Finally he decided that no one had detected his coming. He reached out his hand to grasp the door hatch, and, with one last scan for possible observers, he slipped into the interior of the pod and closed the hatch thankfully behind him.

Fortunately, there was no crew for him to worry about. The pod/powerbarge complex was controlled entirely from a father ship, and all operations were automatic. His only duty was to fasten the dogs of the door hatch securely and check the integrity of the vacuum seals. That done, he activated the "readiness" signal and glanced at his watch. He had barely made the deadline.

A rose-colored light signaled the father ship's acknowledgment of his entry, and he turned his attention to the contents of the dimly lit pod, which was a detachable container positioned under the powerbarge itself. He discerned that the boxes, bales, and packages were all of a standard set which formed the traditional provisions of a hopeful colonist who, shunning the doubtful advantages of living on an exploited star world, was determined to join one of the newer star colonies. Such enterprise found favor with the star kings, because whenever such a development was successful it added one more populated planet to the list of those available for spoil or conquest.

Behind the bales and sacks, Bogaert found something he had not been expecting. Hearing a slight sound, he had crept stealthily around a clump of sacks and found himself suddenly facing a woman, a youth, and a girl child—all regarding him with a hushed apprehension which hinted at much fear of discovery. It was a finding which puzzled him considerably.

Space-riding in barges was an arduous and frequently dangerous experience. Although pressurized with a breathable atmosphere for livestock transport and simplification of cargo handling, the pods were not intended for human occupation. The controls were "ghosted" by a remote farther ship controlling the barge fleet, and the system was not specifically designed to maintain flight stresses within the range of human tolerance. The bribes which had been extended to allow Bogaert to use this harsh mode of exodus from Ortel were a measure of the urgency with which Commissioner Rounding had vested the affair. If a woman and two children had been submitted to a similar risk, it was presumably an expression of a similarly extreme necessity.

His attempt to open conversation provoked such an alarmed reaction that he thought it kinder not to persist. As the counting light indicated the approach of liftoff, however, he became alarmed by their apparent ignorance of how brutal powerbarge acceleration could be. With less than two minutes to go, he strode to their section of the pod, ordered them to lie on the softest materials available, and showed them the posture best suited to resist acceleration pressures. Probably because of the military tone of his commands, they obeyed without argument, and nestled into hollows in the giant sacks which Bogaert released from the clamps and toppled to the deck. With a final check to insure that everyone had sufficient spinal support, Bogaert regained his own place with only seconds to spare before the powerbarge's engines wound into thundering life.

The liftoff was quite as vicious as he had anticipated. The crushing acceleration forced him painfully into the improvised couch, and was maintained in varying degrees of intensity for nearly an hour. This meant that the powerbarge was not being placed in parking orbit for collection with the rest of the barge fleet, but was being accelerated straight toward a high-level hyperdrive condition. It was the first indication he had received that the father ship exercising ghost control of the powerbarge had been merely passing Ortel at some cosmic range and speed and had not been in planetary orbit, as was normal.

The pressures eased abruptly at the onset of hyperpoint. Bogaert's immediate concern was for the safety of the others as the cargo began to redistribute itself to accommodate the vagaries of the crude system of artificial gravity. He was preparing the cargo clamps when he again came face to face with the woman, and he was transfixed by the bright green of her eyes, the perfection of her skin, her honey-gray hair wisping out from under the sternness of the widow's cowl. Here was a vision of the purest nobility—not the grief-stricken widow he had imagined, but a creature who proclaimed royalty with every movement of her immaculate hands. Behind her, the two children watched the encounter with distinct unease.

"You probably saved our lives." Her accent was of one of the far worlds, uncontaminated by Ortellian slur. "I should know your name if you're to be rewarded when the time's proper."

Bogaert smiled and shook his head.

"There's no question of reward, nor could I accept if you gave it me. However, the name's Bogaert, Colonel Bogaert, of the Federation Space Service, latterly attached to Terran Outspace Technical Aid. Everyone calls me Bogey."

A look of relief crossed her brow. "Terran? I feared you might be one of the Pretender's men."

"Hardly! But you, ma'am? This is no way to be traveling with children."

"I know what you mean, Colonel. But circumstances force the issue. You'll forgive my not explaining further."

"No need for explanations. I've already guessed you

to be Miram, the Empress Kanizar. And this" —he turned to where the young girl was regarding him with dubious eyes— "would be Princess Arma. The young fellow with the ion gun must be Prince Zim, heir to most of the galaxy. It seems I travel in august company."

"You're well informed, Colonel . . . er . . . Bogey."

"I merely put the pieces together. I was told you'd fled to Ortel to escape the Pretender. That would explain your presence in Tenarensor. And I presume that you, like myself, are attempting to transship to Terra by the quiet route out of the star kingdoms."

She was examining him curiously. He stopped speaking, perturbed by the intensity of her gaze.

"I'm sorry" she said. "But I confess I've never met a Terran before. I find you difficult to gauge. Why should you need a quiet route out of the star kingdoms? I thought Terrans feared nobody."

"I was cast as the star turn in a survival game organized by Lords Xzan and Oontara. Such engagements are forbidden by protocol. I'm being sent home, out of the way."

"You're running away?" The notion clearly troubled her.

"Effectively. But the principles at stake are more important than the man."

"More important than the honor of a warrior?"

"Terra doesn't have warriors in your sense, Lady Miram. We fight and progress more as a species, not so much as individuals."

"Like ants?" There was suddenly a terrible apprehension in her eyes, which she conquered by an effort of will. "Forgive me, Colonel Bogey! That was an inexcusable remark."

"On the contrary, quite understandable. Coming from your background, you have a natural repugnance for the warrior who runs. I had to make a similar if opposite adjustment when I first encountered the star legions. But what you read as weakness is part of Terra's strength."

"How can it be strength?"

"Because we're as strong as the sum of the parts, not only as strong as the weakest link in the chain. It's a difference of philosophy, not capability. We choose not to fight unless we have to, but that doesn't mean we can't fight when we must. Several star kings have lost their crowns because they couldn't appreciate that fact."

"I suppose that's what they call the new logic. I fear I'll never understand it.'

"It's the old logic to us. It clawed us out of the jungle and into space in less than a million years. It gave us a thriving Federation instead of a miserable set of colony worlds. In a few years more it'll give us access to as many galaxies as this galaxy has stars."

Miram burst into laughter, so suddenly that the children were alarmed. The handgun sprang into Zim's fingers as if it had acquired life of its own. Miram's hand went out to touch Bogaert's wrist in the familiar Meon mode of greeting, and she drew back her cowl and let the honey-gray tresses fall about her neck.

"I wronged you, Colonel Bogey. Not even Kam Kanizar can make such claims. You've proven a vital point. He always says, 'Never get into an argument with a Terran—because the universe is on their side.' Today I appreciate what he means."

The young Prince Zim had witnessed all this with a general lack of comprehension. One thing was certain, however: he greatly disapproved of a painted warrior who spoke to his mother as though to an equal. Holding the gun prominently, he indicated that the Colonel should fall back. Bogaert took his measure sagely, a glint of humor nestling in the corners of his eyes.

"There are several good reasons for not taking that attitude," he said softly. "First, I wish you no harm, rather the reverse. Second, you couldn't fire that thing in here without puncturing the hull and killing us all. Third, you've the safety ring turned the wrong way . . ."

Momentarily the boy looked down to check the accuracy of the last statement. In that split second, Bogaert struck the weapon from his hand and sent it in a long arc into a clump of sacks.

"And fourth, you've got a hell of a lot to learn before you threaten another's life."

Before the Prince could recover from his surprise, Bogaert had recovered the weapon and was offering it back.

"You're a good lad, Zim! Full marks for motivation. But there are a couple of things you need to know about survival through arms: the weaknesses of your enemies—and the strengths of your friends. If ever you point that gun at me again, it had better be with intent to kill. Because if you don't kill me, I swear I'll take it and use it on you."

The Prince's anger and frustration quieted when he read the concern in his mother's eyes. He took the weapon and returned it to his belt. Then, at Miram's unspoken prompting, he extended his hand to touch the Colonel's wrist.

"That's better! Do you realize this old cargo pod holds just about the most wanted selection of people in the galaxy right now? Between us, we've more than sufficient enemies without having quarrels among ourselves."

Tiring of the monotony of the flight, the children began to argue. Miram quieted them and told them to try to sleep. They did not find this easy, but gradually grew silent. Meanwhile, Miram and Bogaert continued talking in low voices. She was apprehensive about the reception she would meet on Terra.

"But what if the Terran authorities won't accept us? After all, Kanizar has no treaty with Terra."

"Nor needs one. You don't need a treaty to extend a principle of common humanity."

"What a strange people you are! Suppose the Pretender threatens reprisals?"

"It won't affect the issue. There's no circumstance that could make Terra hand over a woman and children to a murderer."

"It's nearly beyond belief. Such a thing couldn't happen on a star world."

"That's why Terra won't become a star world. As

Commissioner Rounding says, we're cursed with being unique."

"A curious claim—but one I come to believe."

They continued talking for a while longer, Bogaert gradually managing to allay her fears. Then he held up his hand.

"The transfer to the starship will be tiring and demanding. We should break jump in about three hours from now. I suggest you get a little rest. I'll wake you in good time."

Miram nodded gratefully. A little happier about her future prospects, she joined her children on the sacks, while Bogaert wedged his back into a niche in the wall and listened to the eerie song of hyperspace reverberating around the hull. Soon he permitted himself to doze, knowing that the cessation of the song would wake him.

When he did wake, it was with a start. He looked disbelievingly at his watch. The continuing song of hyperspace swiftly led him to conclude that something was terribly wrong. They were already many hours past rendezvous, and still traveling at megalight velocity.

He did not wake Miram immediately, preferring to first think out the implications of the situation. The answers were anything but encouraging. From the time they had been traveling, they must by now be a great distance from the starliner route and well into one of the less-charted sectors. Here were the great wilds of the galaxy, the haunts of star brigands and the lesser lords, who were forced to take their pickings in the less-desirable areas away from the great star empires. These were the wastelands of space . . . He swore softly.

The sudden sound woke Miram, who came over to him.

"Are we nearly there, Colonel Bogey?"

"I'm afraid not. This old tub's been in hyperspace far too long. I don't know where the hell it's taking us, but I'll guarantee it's not to rendezvous with any starliner."

"Where, then?" She read the concern in his face.

"At a rough guess, Oontara's made a monkey out of Commissioner Rounding. I think we're all in a trap which was set for me. We're going to get the chance to play Xzan's survival game."

Miram looked back at the children, who were just beginning to stir. "Is there nothing we can do?"

"I wish I knew."

Bogaert climbed up a high stack of bales and started to examine a hatch in the ceiling. It was typical of constructions based on *ransad* technology, and he estimated that it could be easily opened if he could improvise a latch manipulator from pieces of colonist's gear. He returned to the floor and began to break open boxes of stores.

"What's up there?" asked Miram uneasily.

"It's a double hatch which couples this pod to the powerbarge proper. There's a sort of test cabin used for setting up instruments before handing over to ghost control. *Ransad* technology's still much of a mystery to me, but there's just a chance I can break the father ship's hold as soon as we fall below hyperpoint."

"I'm afraid I don't understand the technicalities."

"If I can't get control of the powerbarge, it'll probably jettison this pod, with us inside it, at the site of the survival game."

"Oh!"

"If the rumor's correct, the stakes are very high in this game. Conditions will be as near lethal as possible. I'd guess we're to be dumped on one of the uninhabitable worlds where the natural conditions are extreme. So we need everything we can get from the situation to give us a chance of survival. Primarily, we need the powered section of this barge."

Among the stores he found some alloy rods. With a couple of these and a cargo clamp, he fashioned a crude tool with which to attack the hatch lock. Fortune was with him, and he hit on the optimum dimension with a minimum of readjustment. The hatch opened into a hemispherical cabin entirely lined with instrument cells and mechanisms based on *ransad* principles. Climbing the wall rings, he was surprised at how much room was available in the cabin. Because of the differing technological emphasis of the *ransad,* the cramped, closed confines characteristic of Terran utilitarian space technology were absent from this dome. Only the hatch, opening centrally through the floor, prevented it from forming a reasonably habitable cabin.

Translation of the *ransad* into Terran-usable terms was well advanced in Terran circles. Like all Terran outspace personnel, Bogaert had been tutored in the basics of the alien science. He had little difficulty understanding the readings presented by the instrument cells, but comprehension of the complete system was a different matter. He therefore worked by a process of elimination, discarding the elements which were of no immediate concern and concentrating on the sections which appeared to relate to the power, hyperdrive, and subhyperpoint navigation.

The process took a very long time indeed. He was acutely conscious that the task of snatching control away from the ghost was nearly beyond his technical capabilities. The *ransad* ghost, unlike radio control, was an organic, empathic coupling, not designed to be rejected from the receiving end. In any case, he dared risk no imbalance of conditions until the barge's velocity fell below hyperpoint.

The only food available was a little provided by Manu Kan for the short journey to the space rendezvous, and the emergency pack from Bogaert's holdall. They shared it sparingly, not knowing how long the journey might now continue. As the hours stretched into days, both food and water became critically short. Desperately the Kanizars searched the colony stores, and found a small stock of grain biscuits and a container of insipid wine. Though the find was small, it was nonetheless very welcome.

Meanwhile, Bogaert persisted in his attempt to unravel the functions of the *ransad* controls. Periodically Miram would come up to the cabin to see how he was progressing. Normally she accepted his quiet assurances without question, but at last she was driven to voice her fears.

"Is it going to be possible, Colonel Bogey?"

"Possible but dangerous."

"Isn't any risk justified by the alternative?"

"If I interfere with the controls at the wrong moment, it'll kill us more swiftly than any planetary exposure."

She shrugged, and her green eyes burned into his. "If the gods so will it, that's how it must be. Can I do anything to help?"

"Strip out as much sacking and soft things as you can find. Bring them up here and spread them on the floor. When I try to get control, the father ship may detect it and jettison the pod prematurely. It's safer with all of you up here in the cabin, with as much cushioning as possible."

He turned back to the instrument cells, and quickly noted a continuing fall of activity on a unit he thought reported the velocity of the barge falling toward the hyperpoint threshold. Soon the changed note of the hyperspace song told his ears the same message. The journey was coming to an end.

"Speed it up, down there! Five minutes at most."

By way of answer, the young Prince Zim bobbed up through the hatch and shouldered in a large bundle of soft sacking. He climbed through the opening and distributed his burden on the floor, then turned to help his sister with a smaller load. Miram came last, disheveled by her exertions, bringing the largest bundle of all. Bogaert kicked the wraps clear of the hatch and closed it, sealing them off from the pod. The children and the cloths under his feet impaired his mobility, and his understanding of the controls was still far from complete, but he had made as ready as the situation would allow.

As the velocity fell toward hyperpoint, he experimentally tested the reaction of the powerbarge to his own set of controls. His interference was sensed immediately by the father ghost. Alarms sprang up all over the cells. He had betrayed his hand prematurely, but given himself the chance to know and counter some of the measures which could be used against him when he made the final bid. He managed to cancel most of the alarms and inactivate the associated cells. Again he tried the controls. This time he began to feel a firm and definite response, and a momentary hopefulness came over him.

As the ship passed through a low-level hyperpoint, the curious *ransad* soft-screens came alight, displaying pictorially the details of a planetary approach. The *ransad* screens were a fascinating combination of three-dimensional imagery and mobile diagrams, giving a real-time indication of alternative approach modes, the details of which were already set into the instruments. Bogaert chose a different mode from that selected by the ghost, and felt the controls rebel against his fingers. He fought the cells vigorously, returning the mode to the one of his own choice whenever the ghost appeared to reestablish control. Finally the ghost let him have his own way, and soon he could hear the scream of rarefied atmosphere against the hull as the ship made a raw descent toward what the screens told him was a planet called Avida.

In the last instant, the ghost clawed back, and Bogaert momentarily lost control. The careful flight path of the mode was disrupted at a critical stage. The barge, caught between opposing commands, swung like a pendulum. A sea of green forest far below swung crazily across the screens, and the barge threatened to topple into a powered dive assisted by the force of gravity. Bogaert swore, and reset his mode commands in a frenzy, fearing they were too near touchdown to be saved. Miraculously, the barge responded. It steadied, with a dramatic reduction in velocity.

Then the barge made contact with the forest. The pod smashed against a series of springy treetops, and the whole ship spun and lurched and finally slithered with ungainly force down through a tangle of branches. Bogaert was thrown on top of the Kanizars, and all of them rolled into a knot of tangled bodies as the grounding came. Instantly the ghost signaled for the power-barge to jettison the pod and blast off again into space, but the command came a tenth of a second too late. Bogaert's foot kicked in the emergency cell which controlled the power plant, and with the onset of the power shutdown the barge merely shuddered ineffectively before it settled to rest on the forest floor.

EIGHT

Transcending the sounds of nature, a rising scream warned Bethschant that a spacecraft was making planetfall in his vicinity. He searched the cloudless skies for some moments before his sharp eyes found the dot of the spacebarge in powered descent. Even from a distance, it was obvious that something was wrong. The smooth trajectory of the landing mode was interrupted more than once, and the craft drifted far from its intended landing spot. It was traveling nearly horizontally when it passed out of his sight across the swamplands. His sensitive ears failed to pick up the sounds of the final crash, but it was no surprise to Bethschant that the powerbarge failed to rise again, as had been intended.

A gleam of wicked intelligence widened his apelike eyes. On this mission, he had two imperatives: to survive and to insure that the Colonel did not survive. The latter command caused him little concern. Survival on Avida was a full-time profession, and one to which you needed to be born. An outworlder injured in a space crash stood virtually no chance at all. When he had made his own position secure, Bethschant considered, it would be prudent to prove that the Terran had died. A swampland crossing, however, was not to be undertaken without careful preparation, and time was on his side.

His occupation for the first part of the day had been to scout for a good position in which to establish a tree camp. He located a few of the rare species of trees which did not exude an acid sap. Of these, only one had sufficient height and stood far enough from its neighbors to offer the necessary degree of safety. With the agility of a Terran ape, Bethschant began to explore the great plant from bole to branch tip, looking for nests of bite-wings, or the pencil-slim flesh beetles, which could burrow into a body as fast as they could run along a branch.

As he gradually climbed to the higher branches under the great leafed canopy, Bethschant felt himself returning to the ways of his youth. There came slowly back to him his previous understanding of the violent ecology of Avida, in which every living thing needed to regard every other as a mortal enemy. The jaw, the claw, the thorn, the sting, the selective poison, and the razor-edged leaf or scale all had a purpose for both offense and defense. Kill or be killed was the simple law, and this precept was taken to an extreme almost unparalleled anywhere else in the galaxy.

In a cracked branch some fifteen meters above the ground, he located a nest of bite-wings. These flying carnivores, with piranhalike ferocity, had been known to completely devour the carcass of a man within five minutes of the swarm's settling. Smoking out the nest would have been useless, because the swarm would reform locally and remain a constant danger. Instead, he climbed again to the ground and patiently hunted an immature running-horn which had been foolish enough to stray from its herd. Poisoning the freshly-killed carcass with strips of a certain bark pressed into incisions in the flesh, he hoisted the deadly gift on a length of creeper and swung back into the great tree.

From a convenient point above the bite-wing nest, he lowered the carcass gently into the cracked branch and prayed that the occupants of the nest would be content with the bait rather than come out to explore the cause of the disturbance. He was fortunate. After an initial sortie, during which they failed to discover him on the branch above, the bite-wings swarmed back into their hole to feast on the warm, unearned meal. An hour later, Bethschant knew the trick had been successful and felt it was safe to continue his exploration of the tree.

So far as he could tell, there were no flesh beetles present, and the only sting-wings he saw were merely cruising past. High up, he chanced upon a cradle of branches well suited as a sleeping platform. He spent the next few hours scraping away all the bark from the branches of the platform so that the night tendrils were destroyed and would have no chance to penetrate his skin while he slept.

Another worry was a fast-creeper, a parasitic vine which could grow ten meters a day if it chose, and exhibited an almost human intelligence in trapping and securing its prey. The fast-creeper had no roots other than the myriad spines it used to puncture its hosts, whether animal or vegetable; thus, it was impossible to inactivate it completely by attacking any single point. He settled for cutting the vine so savagely and in so many places that he destroyed any coordination it possessed. Some of the fragments continued to reach out for him, but they were clumsy and lacked directional sense, and would not trouble him even if they found him asleep.

Having cleared the worst of the resident perils, it was now necessary to make the tree secure against climbing predators. Rawthorns grew close by, like an entanglement of barbed wire. Though he hurt himself attempting to cut some loose, he soon had a sufficient barrier to encircle the bole of the tree to the height of several men. His own route for entering and leaving the tree was along one vast overhanging bough, and this he trimmed so that nothing could reach it which was less agile than himself. Even then, he took aloft a string of rawthorn with which to seal the branch during the night.

With the resident and climbing predators now taken care of, he needed protection against visiting flying things. To this end, he built a small fire on the forest floor well under the canopy of the tree. Once it was established, he heaped on it quantities of selected bark and roots, and let the heavy aromatic smoke rise to fill the spacious cavity beneath the leafy ceiling. Judicious damping and a good supply of bark would enable him to keep the fire smoldering all night, and its heavily scented smoke would deter most of the nocturnal winged beasties that might otherwise stray into his camp.

Finally he looked up and surveyed his handiwork

proudly. When tied onto the sleeping platform in the high branches amidst the curls of slowly drifting smoke, he would experience the nearest approach to safe sleeping which Avida had been known to offer. There was something immensely satisfying about taking a piece of raw nature and fashioning it into a tolerable habitat with his own knowledge and the skill of his own hands. A stirring from the depths of his ancestry told him it was for such as this that man had been created. This slight deflection of attention nearly cost him his life.

Like a streak of black lightning, something launched itself from a high place behind him. Bethschant sensed its presence too late, and knew of its movement only by the swift passage of a shadow across his path. Desperately he threw himself aside, knowing that the yellowed razor claws missed him by no more than the depth of the fine hairs on his body. Unable to alter its course in mid-flight, the beast continued on its trajectory until it touched the ground, then turned again to the attack, almost faster than the eye could follow—but still too slowly. It ran breast-on into Bethschant's spear blade, and such was the force of the meeting that the shaft penetrated nearly halfway into its body. Its brain was still insisting that the fight was not lost when it toppled, dead, in the path.

Amazed and shaken by the speed and unexpectedness of the encounter, Bethschant inspected his prize. It was a sleek, black, sinuous animal with a body weight twice his own. He did not recognize the species, but the wickedly carnivorous teeth and terrible claws proclaimed it well suited to the role of successful predator. The smooth black pelt and hint of atrophied wings suggested that this was probably another of the continually mutating creatures that came out of the badlands of the north. This was confirmed by the spots of blood and saliva which shone with unnatural luminescence in the shade beneath the brush. He backed away hastily, knowing that the carcass meat would be dangerous to eat. Reluctantly he left his spear, hopelessly embedded in the creature's body, and went to hunt his supper with the aid of a short bow and a knife.

Later, victorious if rather bruised by an encounter with a dominant female running-horn that had tried to defend her plump suckling, Bethschant tied himself happily to the high branches and plastered his skin with sticky leaves to ward off the worst of the airborne sap which drifted from neighboring trees. With a full stomach, the sweet taste of blood on his lips, and the aromatic smoke curling around his nostrils, he reflected that he had had a very successful day. The lure of the old life, demanding though it was, had no counterpart in all the halls of Xzan. It could be easy to forget that the star worlds existed, and drift back into the eternal and continuing challenge that was the way of life on Avida. Sadly, however, he knew that he could not survive for long without a tribal group, nor was there much point in trying to do so without a mate and a chance to perpetuate his seed.

Yet the call of Avida was strong, and Bethschant rested more content that night than he had for several years. Tomorrow—or the day after—he would start to collect materials to build a raft to cross the swamp and look for the Terran. For this night, however, he embraced the old gods of Avida. There was a harmony in the ritual which strengthened the ties between him and his old mother planet, and as the two became one in his consciousness, he drifted into a deep and dreamless sleep.

NINE

Such was the will of the strange gods of Avida that the flight path of the crashing spacebarge had been changed to an almost horizontal direction in the seconds before the actual crash. Despite the conflict over the vessel's trajectory, the reaction drive had remained operating, and the built-in safety circuits had striven to keep the stresses within safe limits. The vessel's remaining momentum had been spent in random brushes with the springy tops of high trees, modifying the landing and cutting a broad swath in the high foliage which marked the line of its progress to its final dropping point. The barge had then slithered down through a nest formed by four tall and resilient trees, only tens of meters from a torn and rocky outcrop which would otherwise certainly have destroyed both ship and occupants.

Even so, their survival was a miracle. Sorting himself out from the tangle of wraps and bodies, Bogaert anxiously noted that Miram and the children appeared to have suffered no more than minor injuries. He wrestled with the hatch, opened it, and peered down into the pod. Most of the clamps had broken open, and the heap of torn cargo was a grim pointer to what might have happened to anyone remaining below. The *ransad* space-alloy hull had been extensively buckled by its bruising passage through the treetops, and in one area a huge tear left a gap large enough to admit the body of a man. Nevertheless, the protective outriggers of the powerbarge had kept the whole structure approximately vertical, and, wedged as they were between the trees, there was no fear that the assemblage might topple.

Bogaert climbed down into the pod, scrambled across the broken stores, and peered out through the rent in the hull. He was faced by an alienly beautiful forest scene, which showed their present position to be on a slight slope which ran gently down to where he could discern a hint of black, as if of swampland water. The whole scene was vibrant with life, and the foliage was vivid with incredible blooms. This planet had been chosen for the survival game, however, and Bogaert had no illusions about the probable dangers inhabiting the apparently peaceful forest strip. If Xzan and Oontara had wagered whole space territories on his ability to survive such a place, it was likely to be a very tough proposition—especially with a woman and two children, encumbrances which the gamblers had not foreseen.

Miram followed him down, assisting the descent of Prince Zim, who had an open cut on his forehead.

"Water—can you find us any water? And ointment?"

Bogaert looked wryly around the wrecked pod.

"There may be a medicine kit buried under that lot somewhere, but it'll take a while to find. Tamp the blood flow with some clean cloth, and let the clot seal itself. We have more important things to do first."

"Leave the blood on his face?" Miram was aghast.

"Time to clean it later. He won't die if it doesn't get infected. Until we know what the local water's like, we don't dare risk using it for anything. Better all of you start sorting these stores. We must know what our assets are before nightfall."

He waited for Arma to descend. She had been crying, and his heart went out to her, but there were many important things to be done and little time in which to do them.

Thrusting his way back up into the cabin, he turned his attention to the state of the power plant and the damaged cell by which he had terminated its activity. He found the situation worse than he had feared. The impact of the crash landing had virtually closed the plant down. Less than a millionth of its original power was still available, and there was no provision for its reactivation in the field. His hopes fell considerably, because he knew too well the value of an efficient power supply in aiding survival under adverse conditions.

Stripping the cells from around the power plant was not an easy job, and he did it only to find out whether it was possible for the unit to be reactivated. After a struggle, he managed to gain access to the incredibly small power plant itself, which harnessed some obscure principle of relativity to permit mass-to-energy conversion with a power-to-weight ratio still undreamt of by Terrestrial technology.

He knew that the shutdown of the power plant had been designed in as a safety feature to prevent the destructive liberation of its vast potential in the event of a disaster. He also knew that the attention of skilled *ransad* technicians could restore it to working order. Unfortunately, his knowledge of that aspect of the alien technology was severely limited. Although he understood the basic principles of the method, he had neither the tools nor the training to perform the operation. The only power he was able to draw from it was electricity for the emergency lighting, which, by translating the Ortellian nameplate, he found had a value of about twelve Terran volts of direct current.

At this point it occurred to Bogaert that no sounds were coming from the pod below, where the Kanizars were supposed to be sorting the stores. With a sudden fear, he descended the rings and found Arma alone, gazing fearfully through the rent in the hull.

"Where's your mother and Zim?"

"They went out—to get water. Zim's hurt his head."

"Hell!" Bogaert looked for the nearest available weapon, which proved to be an Ortellian ax, and forced his way through the rent. "Which way did they go?"

"Down there." Arma pointed the way through the brush to where a slight clearing permitted a gleam of black water to show against the vivid forest green. Forgetting discretion, Bogaert broke into a fast sprint toward the point where even now he could hear Miram's voice rising in panic.

"Zim! Zim! What've I done?"

Some camouflaged animal moved under Bogaert's flying feet. He continued running, reflecting that if the creature were going to attack, it would already have done so. Moments later, he plunged down a bank and found Miram and Zim. The boy was staggering away from his mother, his hands covering his face, issuing frightened screams and moans.

"What happened?" Bogaert swung Miram around roughly.

"I tried to bathe his face with this."

She held up a metal container full of what appeared to be dirty water. Closer inspection showed that it writhed with a mass of hair-fine worms whose ends even now probed out of the water and attempted to reach her shaking hands.

Bogaert seized Zim and wrenched the boy's hands away from his face. As he feared, many dozens of the worms had penetrated the flesh and were even now thickening and reddening as they sucked the living blood. Swearing impiously, Bogaert looked around for something which would burn. A dry, golden bush suggested itself as useful material. He tore off a few twigs and ignited them in the discharge gap of his pocket igniter. They flared readily and, when rubbed between his fingers, continued to smolder.

He applied a glowing splint to each of the reddening worms, and was gratified to find that each contracted with a spasm and fell away, leaving only a small red mark in the skin. So fine and so numerous were the worms that it took him many minutes to be sure he had removed them all. When he was finished, he turned his attention to Miram, who had gone into a tearful frenzy, trying to brush the worms from her own arms and hands. Soon she too was free of the creatures, and her frightened sobbing began to abate. She turned to him gratefully.

"Bogey, I—"

"Later," said Bogaert. "Let's get back to the ship. Arma's alone, and I don't think we've seen the worst of what's out here."

He picked up the container of water and, holding it carefully by its base, his fingers out of range of the probing hair-worms, he led the way back to the stricken barge. Zim followed, pale and shaken, his face a mass of red blotches in addition to his original cut, but apparently otherwise unharmed. Miram, her arms bare and delicately pale, seemed to find something new troubling her skin, and looked constantly and apprehensively up into the great trees, as if seeking the source of the irritation.

Bogaert noticed something stinging his wrists and neck. His keen eyes detected slight aerosol droplets, revealed in a shaft of sunlight viewed against shade. These liquid particles were apparently being exuded from the heights of the giant trees, and their action was a strong irritant to human skin. Whether its effect would be mild or persistent he had yet to learn, but the idea of a constant rain of alien fluid filled him with strong and private fears.

Before they were halfway along the path, Arma's piercing scream cleaved the air. With his ax raised, Bogaert charged forward, to be confronted by a fantastic creature like a large armor-clad rat which sat snarling in the rent in the pod wall. At the sound of his approach, the creature whirled to face him, with a speed faster than Bogaert's eyes could follow, and its scorpionlike tail twitched in a blur. The Colonel viewed the teeth and claws warily, and knew the creature's reaction speed precluded any sane attempt to attack it with the ax.

Zim stopped at his side, drew his ion gun, and sighted it at the creature. Then, to insure no possibility of missing, he advanced a couple of paces before squeezing the trigger. There was a click, but the weapon failed to fire. In a blur of flying legs and snapping jaws, the creature hurled itself across the intervening distance straight at Zim's throat.

By some gift of inspiration, Bogaert's ax stroke intercepted the hurtling body in mid-flight, and the ax blade bit deeply into the soft flesh under the armor plate. A blue fluid spurted from the wound and spattered Bogart's arms as he followed the stricken body to the ground and hacked at it until most of its limbs were severed and its life gone.

Meanwhile, Miram had run on to a tearful reunion with her frightened daughter, and Zim, wan and aghast, was looking at the weapon which had failed him. Wiping the blue life fluid of the creature from his arms in some disgust, Bogaert motioned the boy into the pod and followed with his face as stern as thunder.

"A stright word, Miram. If you'd done as I'd asked, none of this would have happened. Instead, we've all four been at risk without any gain. Don't underestimate this place. Its choice was no accident. So until the three of you learn how to survive under these conditions, you're going to damn well have to take orders—my orders."

"Nobody gives orders to Kanizars." Zim rose swiftly to his mother's defense. "Least of all painted warriors."

"To me, you aren't Kanizars. You're a family in need of protection. That won't be easy to provide, so I'm going to tell you something you'll forget at your peril. The next one who wanders off without permission takes the consequences alone. I won't risk the group again to save an individual. Is that clearly understood?"

The assent was nodded rather than spoken. Bogaert scowled and held out his hand. "Now let me see that ion gun."

Zim surrendered the weapon meekly. Bogaert drew it apart and examined the mechanism.

"Must have been damaged in the crash. The control-store's fractured. I can set it for single shots, but after each shot it'll take about ten minutes to recharge. If you have to use it, better not miss. You might not get a second chance."

A cry from Miram brought a sudden shift of attention.

"Something's burning my skin."

"And mine," said Zim.

"Arma?"

"No-o."

"Then it must be the droplets from the big trees. I thought it was too clean beneath them."

"Too clean?" queried Miram.

"Yes. No dead vegetation or anything left rotting. I'd guess the trees are dropping some sort of digestive enzyme—something which converts dead organic matter quickly into food for the roots."

"You mean it's sort of eating us?"

"Trying to."

"But we aren't dead," protested Zim.

"The outer layers of our skin is. Likewise hair and nails." He examined the growing redness of Miram's arms and looked at his own. "Mine's a lot less where that creature's blood splashed me. Which suggests the enzyme's water-soluble. Spit on our arms and wipe it off with a cloth till I see what I can do about the water from the swamp."

"But that water's no good," said Miram. "It's got those things in it. And what are we going to drink?"

"Start working your way through those stores again.

Look particularly for food, weapons, tools, and medicines. Zim, you come help me with the water."

"But the worms . . ." The lad touched his face anxiously.

"Given the water, we'll find a way of dealing with the worms. Now everybody get busy. We've a lot to do before nightfall, and we've lost a lot of time already."

Bogaert took his ax, and Zim his ion gun. Very warily this time, the two of them moved off through the clearing toward the dark water. After his recent outburst, Zim had accepted the Terran's leadership without further question. Now he was becoming curious about the alien Colonel who had no awe of Kanizars.

"Don't Terrans ever carry guns?"

"Frequently we do—but not when we're supposed to be on duty in friendly territory. It might give the wrong impression. We don't dare risk being confused with warriors."

"What's wrong with warriors?"

"Warriors destroy—but only man creates. Destruction's a negation of all that makes man unique."

"If that's what they call the new logic, I don't think much of it. I'll be a warrior, like my father."

"And I've no doubt you'll be a good one. But by the time you've conquered the galaxy, Terra will have conquered the intergalactic drive. We'll have access to as many galaxies as you'll have access to stars. So whose logic is the stronger?"

The boy obviously considered this a piece of homespun idiocy, and crouched like a wary protector to cover Bogaert as he took cans to the edge of the water and filled them.

This was the first time that Bogaert had had a close view of the swamp. The sight impressed him only with a feeling of hopelessness. Both the depths and the surface of the water were alive with life in constant conflict. Fantastic insects darted and preyed on the water dwellers and were themselves picked out of the air by leaping serpents' tongues or fast-flying scavengers; even the well-armored and the quick probably survived as a species more by virtue of fast breeding than by any advantage in attack or defense. The whole pattern of life boded no good for any species late maturing or with a long gestation period. Small wonder that, on Avida, man had not achieved his usual dominance.

Now that he was conscious of the pitch of the life-and-death struggle, Bogaert began to discern evidence of it on all sides. Nothing was neutral. It was a pattern of kill or be killed, eat or be eaten, multiply or become extinct. Individuals had no value except for their contribution to the food chain. Survival was a continuing battle against the most staggering odds, and death was the penalty for a moment of inattention. If there was a moral to be learned from his observations, it was that the only sure method of defense was continued and unremitting attack.

Their return to the pod was uneventful, but Bogaert's face grew increasingly stern when he saw the nature of the stores. The colonist's kit had been "edited." The basic survival rations intended to take a colonist through the acclimatization period had been omitted; likewise the weapon pack, the water-treatment plant, fuel pellets, and the medicine bags. The remaining stores consisted of seeds and dry beans, agricultural instruments, materials, tools, and an assortment of *ransad* technical pieces which had presumably formed part of some communications package, the rest of which was missing.

Bogaert looked at the dirty, bruised, thirsty, and hungry faces of his companions and back at the poor assortment of things which were their sole possessions. Behind him, something prowled inquisitively close to the rent in the pod wall. The piteous cry of an animal nearby falling into the jaws of an enemy was a pointed comment on the dangers which awaited them. The hairy net of worms reaching out for his fingers over the edge of the water can was a potent reminder that they had not even achieved a source of the barest essentials of life.

"Adaptation's the keynote of survival," said Bogaert reflectively. "Either you adapt to suit your environment, or you adapt it to suit you. I propose to take the latter course. We may never win against Avida, but we're going to have a damn good try. We'll pick up the problems as they come, and concentrate on staying alive. The one spark of hope is Commissioner Rounding. When Hilary finds we're missing, he'll stir the galaxy itself until he finds out where we are."

TEN

As Camin Sher came to count the cost of his attack on Meon, his face grew increasingly sour and his capacity for vengeance increasingly great. The battle had lost him twelve warships, including his own flagship, fully a third of his attack force on this mission, and represented a loss of twenty thousand trained star warriors. That such havoc had been caused by a mere handful of small patrol vessels raised something very bitter in his throat.

Now, however, his target ships had neutralized the fiercest of the ground defenses, and threats of massive destruction had been delivered to the more highly populated areas. Finally, all resistance died. The Pretender ordered his great ships down to strategic points, reserving his present craft and one other to make planetfall on the pads of the twin fortresses of Andor and Ute, which stood between the Field of Perfection and Kanizar's own establishment.

It should have been a proud moment—arriving in triumph to take over the castle of the King of Kings—but the losses had taken the edge off the victory. Something about the final acquiescence of the garrison made Sher nervous in case he was being tricked or cheated. It was therefore with caution and a great deal of unnecessary brutality that the Pretender finally arrived at the throne.

He gave orders that Miram and the Kanizar heirs be brought to him. As was his practice, he offered a rich reward to whoever should succeed in this endeavor. After twelve hours of frustration, he doubled the reward and listened furiously to bearer after bearer of conflicting rumor and speculation, all of which proved to be without foundation. There were no clear clues as to the whereabouts of the Empress Kanizar or her children.

Then somebody made a positive find. Two members of Kanizar's council were located in hiding, and with them was old Sashu, Kanizar's chancellor and confidante. Camin Sher ordered them slowly tortured until they broke and revealed the whereabouts of the missing Kanizars. He himself attended the atrocities, insistent that none should be allowed to die before the truth was known. All three held their secret to the end of their lives. The look of agonized triumph on old Sashu's face as he passed away upset Sher's stomach and completed the sense of defeat in the midst of victory.

By this time circumstantial evidence was being acquired. The destination of a freighter which left just before the Pretender's arrival was found to be Tenarensor on Ortel. That the Empress and her children had gone by this route nobody then bothered to deny. Even with his best ships, Sher could not reach Ortel before the freighter docked, and although the Pretender was tolerated in the realms of Oontara, his visit would be on sufferance and his use of arms forbidden.

Everyone assumed that King Oontara would become Miram's protector, because Sashu's injunction to the contrary had been communicated to none but the Empress herself. In a towering rage, the Pretender ordered his fleet back into space, spurred by his urgent need to destroy the Kanizar heirs and mindful that the mighty Kam Kanizar himself would now be on his way home, hot with vengeance. The garrison mistook Sher's hasty departure for a rout, and rose in armed rebellion, which cost Sher a further thousand warriors. The natural space-borne retribution which such insurrection would normally have earned was foregone by the departing fleet, lest Kanizar's vengeful forces be nearer than they supposed.

When they neared Oontara's star territory, Camin

Sher had his fleet stand well off in space. It was provoc-
ative and dangerous to attempt to take a star fleet into
the territory of a king as powerful as Oontara. Instead,
Sher took a single ship through to the spaceport at Tenarensor and, having been formally identified, was
granted permission to make planetfall. The Pretender
found the protocol galling. He determined, if he succeeded Kanizar, to make Oontara pay for the indignity.
For the moment, however, polite compliance with Oontara's wishes was the surest way to his goal.

Even before he sought an audience with Oontara, the
Pretender contacted his own network of spies and sympathizers, and learned from them two things which improved his hopes considerably. Miram and the Kanizar
heirs had definitely arrived on Ortel and had gone not
to Oontara but to one Manu Kan, a powerful merchant
and friend of Kanizar himself. Second, the Pretender's
own sycophant, the star lord Xzan, was currently visiting Oontara's court, and had the direct ear of the star
king.

Taken together, these two pieces of news pleased
Camin Sher greatly. He had to operate warily while on
Ortellian soil. Oontara was unlikely to countenance the
murder or abduction of Kanizar's kin from his own sovereign territory, but action against the merchant might
be practical if it could be done discreetly. Having Xzan
as a willing ally in the Tenarensor court could be useful
in case things went wrong.

The Pretender sought and was granted an audience
with Oontara. He exchanged star gossip and had rooms
placed at his disposal, but mentioned nothing of the real
purpose of his visit. Oontara, who listened attentively to
every whisper of rumor around his halls, made an astute
guess that the Pretender had not come visiting for social
reasons or for trade. Nevertheless, the star king kept his
ideas to himself, but later summoned Manu Kan, the
merchant, to come to him privately.

"Manu, we've known each other long enough to be
able to speak with the true meaning of words. Therefore, listen to what I have to say. Politics and intrigue

are the concern of kings. I don't sell or barter goods. Why, then, do you meddle in politics?"

"My Lord, I don't think I understand."

"You understand well enough. Why does the Pretender come seeking goods you've no intention of selling?"

Manu Kan was a huge man with a tanned and open face. Behind his apparently simple and picturesque exterior was an experienced and calculating mind fully a match for Oontara's. His initial show of perplexity changed to one of bland relief.

"My Lord, the Pretender wastes his time. The consignment he seeks was but goods in transit. It's long since been transshipped to Terra."

"A strange choice of destination—though I'm glad to hear it. But the Pretender's intelligence is seldom at fault. How come he still seeks goods which are unavailable?"

"With respect, my Lord, commercial security's a tighter school than the whispering galleries of court."

"That's a certainty!" said Oontara heavily. "But repeat the assurance that we've nothing here to interest the Pretender."

"Did I not load the consignment with my own hands? It was very late at night, and there were few who could be trusted with so delicate a task."

"I'll accept that, Manu. But any troubles you meet as a result of playing star politics are troubles you've brought upon yourself. If the Pretender's sympathizers attack you, I grant you right of arms in defense. But don't involve the Ortellian Guard. Officially, none of this ever happened."

"I understand, my Lord Oontara. And thank you for your kind interest in the details of my trade."

"Don't thank me yet. You've strayed into kings' business. I've a mind to teach you a lesson. The cost of whatever complications arise you'll find added to your taxes. Come, Manu, take wine with me. Perhaps tomorrow you'll be able to afford none of your own."

Meanwhile, Camin Sher was making little progress. He soon found that money was insufficient to encourage his sympathizers to attack the strongholds of Manu Kan. The Merchant's reputation for close security and strong defense was almost a legend in Tenarensor, nor was anyone agreed as to which of Manu's establishments might house the missing trio.

In desperation, Camin called on the sycophantic Xzan, who saw in the Pretender a powerful patron in his struggle to win kingship. Xzan was overjoyed to be of service. If the Pretender succeeded in his quest, the sycophant could be in a very favorable position.

"You've already spoken to Oontara?" he asked Sher.

"I spoke guardedly. He's no man to take part in a plot against Kanizar."

"Oontara softens considerably since his flirtation with Terra. He's no longer the star demon we used to know. Have you seen that bark he bought from Terra? A tiny, ornate toy. He could've had a *ransad* warship from his own weapon shops for less than half the price. Thus he buys himself into favor with these whelps and mewlings of the galaxy."

"They call them the terrible infants," said Sher doubtfully. "I'd not care to invoke their wrath. But we stray from the point. What can you find out about the Empress Miram and her litter?"

"Whatever's to be known I'll find. Oontara's lost his craftiness. He talks too much when full of wine. I already know that after your audience with him he called the merchant Manu Kan and they had talks in private. Oontara was not displeased with the result."

"What does that suggest?"

"Seeing how soft Oontara's become, I'd guess Miram and the spawn of Kanizar aren't still on Ortel. With you in Tenarensor and Kanizar soon in pursuit, there's no other circumstance that could make Oontara lie easily in bed."

"That makes sense, Xzan. It also explains why no spies have been able to trace their whereabouts. But if they've left, I must know where they went."

"If Oontara knows—and I suspect he does—we'll

have his secret out. Tonight I fete and feast him. I'll give him wine until his eyeballs show the level of it. I'll lend him my softest concubine, who'll leave him so sated he'll think his manhood's fled. Then he'll talk and have no guard on what he says."

"I should think he'd go to sleep on you. Still, I leave it to you. Find where Miram's gone, and it'll count much store for you."

"I seek no reward, my Lord Sher. Only to be of service to the galaxy's true king."

"I recall you making the same noises once to Kanizar. I prefer intelligent self-interest to loyalty. Loyalties change, but self-interest's a predictable constant."

During the night, the Pretender was awakened by his guards. They brought a drunk and stupefied Xzan to his bedside.

Sher shook him roughly. "What's the answer? Did Oontara speak?"

Xzan swayed mightily, and would have fallen had he not been supported by the soldiers' arms. His voice was thick and infinitely tired.

"Oontara had the evening . . . of his life. Then he said, 'Xzan, old friend . . . I hope you're doing all this for the love of me. If you want to know where the Kanizars have gone, you need only ask. They've gone to Terra. Not even the Pretender can touch them there.' "

"Terra?" This was a blow Camin Sher had not anticipated. No star monarch had ever attacked a Terran installation and escaped without the most hideous of losses. Sher had proved this point at his own cost. Yet the mild-seeming Terrans seemed to bear no enmity, and continued to spread the gospel of federation and the new logic to friend and foe alike. Nor had any spy ring or system of espionage ever made effective penetration of the home planet. Sher sensed that he was beaten, but needed to think about the implications. The swaying Xzan was a positive distraction. Sher motioned to his guard.

"Take him away and lay him somewhere to sleep it off. I'll see him again when he's sober."

The inebriated Xzan, slurring mild protests, was assisted from the room and laid on a couch in the corridor. There his welfare was taken over by a short, fat man in a white suit, named Hilary Rounding, who began inquiring solicitously about the wrongs the day had brought to the noble Lord Xzan.

ELEVEN

From his growing appreciation of the ever-present dangers, Bethschant judged that his acclimatization to Avida was nearly complete. In the past few days he had made very few mistakes, and though he knew complacency was equated with death, he now felt sufficiently confident to abandon his tree camp.

From the top of his tree he had daily surveyed the direction taken by the crashing barge, wondering if it was possible that the Terran Colonel had survived. The prospect seemed unlikely, but Bethschant's own interest prompted him to make the journey to prove the point. In any case, the terms of his assignment made it necessary for him to complete any death-dealing that Avida left unfinished. He therefore turned his attention to gathering materials for the raft he would need to make the journey across the swamp.

Finding cane was no problem. The difficulty lay in finding cane sufficiently dried so that the resin had been driven out to glaze the surface and render it waterproof. Shortly after attaining a suitable level of glaze, the material became susceptible to the acid sap from the trees, and was rapidly digested to a useless fragility. Again and again he risked the razor-sharp leaf edges only to have the precious tubes crumble to powder at his touch.

All day he worked patiently at the task, stopping only to hunt when he saw an easy prospect or to retreat when the natural dangers proved too great. By evening he had most of the cane he needed, and he piled it regretfully on the ground, knowing that by morning much of it would have succumbed to the rot and he would need to start gathering again.

Returning to his tree, he felt a pang of disloyalty to Avida as his thoughts turned longingly to the imperishable boats used on the star worlds. Then something reminded him that his raft was a way of life, whereas a boat was an impersonal ancillary. Few star-worlders outside those who worked in the great black mills had the knowledge or the skill to build their own vessels, and those who did took their methods solely from the *ransad* texts. In contrast, Bethschant's own brain and hands had to supply everything he needed for the job. The gods assured him that he should be proud of being a one-man civilization, and he tied himself to the tree and fell asleep with a smile of honest satisfaction on his face.

In the morning, a rare wind broke the tranquility of the forest, and another creature from the badlands worried his canepile, scenting human flesh but unable to find its location. Bethschant stayed out of the way. The creature was far too powerful to engage in needless combat. Its flesh would be dangerous to eat, so he did not need to kill it for food.

Nevertheless, the creature's visit worried him. This was the third badlands animal he had encountered in five days. Their numbers were increasing, and they were spreading farther south in search of food. This was a radical change from the old days, and a reminder that the remorseless march of evolution had still not produced a dominant animal on Avida. There was a bitterness in Bethschant's heart as he reflected that whereas man had dominance on so many worlds, the human population of Avida had been forced down to an insignificant animal level. The legends had it that this had not always been so, but that the sons of Avida had somehow lost their way in the unending struggle to survive.

After a couple of hours, the creature grew tired of seeking a quarry it could smell but not locate. It finally charged off through the bushes after a fleeting wildfoot, leaving Bethschant to hunt his breakfast and examine his pile of canes. By the time he had made good the overnight wastage and begun to plait his raft, the day was already well advanced, and it was far later than he would normally have considered prudent for such a venture. However, if he delayed another night, even more of his cane would have rotted, and once the plaiting had been started, replacement would be difficult or impossible. Viewing the tall shoulder of an island jutting out of the swamp, he determined to reach at least that far before nightfall.

As soon as the raft was finished, he gathered his possessions together. The spear which he had lost had now been replaced by a shaft which was longer and lighter than the original. He carefully checked the poison on its tip to insure that it was still fresh and active. His other weapons had their appointed places on the raft, where he could find them without an instant's hesitation. The long-knife hung from a plaited girdle around his waist, always within swift reach of his fingers; his precious flints were strung around his neck for safety; and some ribbons of dried meat and half a shell of ash-filtered water made his preparations complete.

With one last wistful look at the tree which had served him so well, Bethschant took up a length of heavy cane and began to push his fragile craft out onto the shallow waters. He immediately became absorbed by the need to find deeper water. Because of the shallow tides, some of the clumps of weedbed were partially submerged, and the thick black water did much to conceal their presence. The task was not eased by the ribbon worms, whose flat external stomachs surfaced in response to any disturbance, giving the appearance of shallows where there were actually depths.

Patiently but persistently, because the sun was growing low, Bethschant leaned to his task. To be trapped on the swamp after nightfall would prove fatal, because the night creatures were even more fearful than those of the day. Long ago in childhood he had lain and listened with dread to the sound of talking-pipe, whose eerie resonance was uncommonly like snatches of human conversation. Legend had it that just before it killed, talking-pipe repeated its victim's name three times. Bethschant was not sure. It had shouted his name quite plainly and often in the night, but had not killed him yet.

Among other nocturnal visitors were the hoverghosts, said to be the hunters of men's souls. Whether they were a single creature or a composite of many was uncertain. These man-sized fluorescent specters floated jauntily over the dark waters, hindered by neither weapon nor brush. It was Bethschant's private speculation that they were swarms of luminous flies. Perhaps it was the terror these apparitions evoked on approach which caused men to leap from safe places, to be swallowed by the swamp. He doubted very much that the ghosts were the harbingers of death, but their ability to locate a frightened man in hiding was something he never could explain.

His present dangers were more tangible, if no less severe. Brilliantly colored sting-wings were everywhere, hovering and darting around the weed clumps. The quantity of poison a single sting-wing could inject was sufficient to cause immediate paralysis in a man. In his path there were literally hundreds, and his surest defense against them was itself a dangerous maneuver.

With a single push of his pole, he directed the raft toward a small sting-wing swarm. Then he took up his long-knife and waited until he had drifted close enough to attract the swarm's notice. When they attacked, he was ready with his knife, striking in a swift pattern which took advantage of the creatures' broad wing span. In seconds, and with an amazing skill, he had dewinged about a dozen, and their bright carcasses, many of them still alive, adorned the platform of the raft. From then on, the sight and smell of the carnage would deter any others, and he was relatively safe from sting-wing attack until the carcasses had dried.

If he was fortunate with the sting-wings, he was less

than lucky with the fibrous swamp life. He was yet only halfway across, and already the fibroid life attached to the underside of the raft had made it heavy and sluggish and dangerously low in the water. Worse still, fine writhing tentacles were beginning to penetrate the plaiting and attack his feet and ankles. He could deal with these blind growths easily enough while he had only them to contend with, but if his attention was diverted by any other danger, they would become a serious menace with their virtually inexhaustible appetite for blood.

A new attack came sooner than he had anticipated, and was nearly fatal. As he was passing over what his pole told him was a particularly deep area of water, he felt something move as the pole struck down. Knowing that he had disturbed and probably angered some sizable water creature, he shelved the pole and snatched up his spear with his right hand, while his left took the knife.

Even thus prepared, he nearly missed the loathsome noduled tentacles which rose silently out of the water behind him and made to encircle his waist. As soon as his alert senses noted the movement of its shadow, he turned on it, hacking with the knife and jabbing with the spear at where he hoped the muscle might be. Crippled and foreshortened, the tentacle fell back, but another twenty rose to grasp the raft in its entirety, and began to crush it as fingers might crush a handful of straw. His only hope lay in the spear with which he probed down, seeking the great creature below and trying to reach some vital point of its body. He met with dangerously little success.

It was unexpected allies which saved him. As the raft was crushed, several dead or near-dead sting-wings were caught between the writhing gray tentacles of the water beast. The paralytic venom was still active, and some of the fluid from their vicious needles penetrated the water beast's flesh. Soon the tentacles slowed and stiffened, leaving Bethschant with the job of trying to extricate the mashed raft from the horrific death-locked fingers.

By the time he had succeeded in this, both he and the

raft were in a very sad state. The raft was waterlogged and barely able to support his weight, all his protective sting-wing carcasses had been washed away, the creeping fibroid tentacles had stripped considerable areas of skin from his ankles, and his blowpipe and throwing stick had floated away. Somehow, by blind force of will and a refusal to be daunted by any further injuries or attacks, Bethschant poled his floating mess toward the island. In the fading light his eyes had spotted a patch of firebushes on the shore, and it was to this point of the island that he desperately worked his way.

It was full darkness as he finally dragged himself through the living slime and up the bank. Fortunately, the firebushes were plentiful and readily responsive as tinder. He dragged a dozen of them out by the roots and threw them together, setting them on fire to sterilize a sleeping place. He pulled out glowing splints from the leaping flames and used them to help dislodge the numerous fleshworms and similar parasites he had acquired on his skin during the crossing. Then he made a filter of crushed embers, treated some swamp water, and drank thirstily while he waited for his sleeping space to become tolerably cool. Rather than cut an overcover, he rolled his sticky, sweating body in the warm gray ash, placed his spear between his knees, ready for instant use, and promptly went to sleep.

So complete was his exhaustion that although talking-pipe called: "Bethschant! Bethschant! Bethschant!" monotonously across the water, and the hoverghosts sought him silently through the bushes, he was aware of none of this. He was a son of Avida, and had done his duty for the day—obeyed the precept to survive. With that done, the gods could ask no more of him. They could repay such fidelity by guarding his journey through to morning's light.

TWELVE

Their first night on Avida had been miserable and critical. Drinking water was their primary need. Straining the water they had collected from the swamp through the finest filter he could improvise, Bogaert obtained an amber liquid certainly too biologically contaminated to be considered for drinking. Outside the pod, he lit a fire and heated some of the strained water in a metal canister. This probably effected some degree of sterilization, but the resultant liquid was salt and sour to the taste, and still not drinkable. He allowed the others to dip their fingers in it when cool and use it to wipe their skins to relieve the intolerable itching caused by the aerosol rain from the trees.

Hunting through the stores which Miram had organized, he found a spouted vessel with a lid, and a length of flexible metal tube. With these he managed to produce a crude and inefficient air-cooled still, but at least the clear liquid which dripped out contained nothing more noxious than rust. By nightfall the apparatus had produced about a large thimbleful of water each—enough to moisten the mouth but not to quench the thirst. Then all the water was gone, and it was too dark and dangerous to make another journey to the swamp that day.

Bogaert encouraged the others to go up into the cabin to sleep, while he took Zim's gun and stayed on guard near the rent in the hull. He occupied the time trying to assess what best he could do to ensure their survival with the facilities available to him. A more efficient and continuous still was his first priority. In this connection, he remembered the electrical output available from the *ransad* power unit. By the dim illumination of the emergency light, he found what appeared to be some resistance wire in one of the *ransad* technical crates. The necessary length of wire would have to be determined empirically, but he was sufficiently confident of the value of the find to go on to construct an air-cooled condenser made out of seed cans, of which he had a reasonable supply. A rough calculation suggested that with this apparatus and a degree of luck, he could probably produce about twenty liters of water a day—enough for at least their immediate needs.

With the others having a sorely-needed sleep, he was reluctant to go up to the cabin to experiment with the electrical part of the system. Instead, he completed the rest of the still as far as he was able. Then he rested on a pile of sacks, intending to remain awake until morning, when he could attempt to free the door hatch, which had become jammed in the crash, and close the rent in the wall. Sleep took him unawares. He woke in a panic as something black and snarling moved sinuously inside the broken hull.

Even in sleep, he had made his hand retain the ion gun, pointing toward the open hole. As his eyes focused, he fired, knowing as he did so that he had only one chance. The whipcrack thunder and flare dazed and blinded him, but the sinuous creature must have divined his intent and escaped a hairsbreadth before the beam struck. His shot drilled a neat hole in the hull but left no carcass to show for the endeavor. Even then, he was not aware how dangerous had been his lapse into sleep until he found that the tip of his left shoe had been sheared off by amazing teeth, missing his toes by an uncomfortably small amount. The dawning shock caused a buzzing in his ears as he contemplated just how sharp the teeth must have been and how incredibly powerful the jaws that drove them. He knew he was more than fortunate to still have a foot.

Zim, disturbed by the noise, had raised the cabin hatch and was peering down anxiously. Miram was looking over his shoulder.

"You all right, Colonel Bogey?"

"Only just." Bogaert knew his voice sounded ragged, but his vocal cords were taut. While he had no wish to alarm them, he was incapable of concealing his shock at the narrowness of his escape from injury. "Better you all stay up there while I check around. There was an animal in here, and it may still be hiding."

"I'll help you."

Despite Bogaert's warning injunction, Zim clambered down the rings. His presence brought a comforting sense of camaraderie to Bogaert. Suddenly he was no longer alone with the problems. His role had been recast as elder of the tribe. Admittedly, it was a very small tribe, but the essential principles remained. Now Zim stood beside him, the younger element, anxious to learn and share in the defense. The others, too, would have their parts to play.

"What're we looking for?" asked Zim.

"Black furry thing about as big as my forearm. I don't know if it's still here or it ran off. We'd better check the stores carefully. Watch out for its teeth."

Waiting for the ion gun to reprime itself, he handed it to Zim and took up an Ortellian long-knife. As they started a wary approach on the stores, a fleeting body, arm-thick and moving with incredible speed, shot out from beneath a sack of beans. Before Zim had had time to raise his useless weapon, Bogaert's knife had cleaved the body into sections. Blood was spattered wide on the yellow sacks.

Almost immediately, a further half dozen of the creatures emerged, burrowing their way out of sacks and boxes with a rapidity which was frightening. Zim discarded his gun and seized an ax. For the next fifteen minutes, the two of them hacked and chopped in the direction of anything that moved, mainly without effect but finally winning the exhausting battle. Examination of the corpses revealed a hairy, tubelike animal with fully a hundred spindly legs and a set of jaws at one end which justified the caution of their approach.

Sweating, and spattered with blood, Bogaert and Zim grinned at each other in triumph. In the course of the battle, they had completely disordered the stores again, and done much incidental damage with their weapons. Bogaert was concerned that the rent in the hull was still open to further intruders, but until he could free the door hatch for human access, he dared not attempt to bend the space alloy back into place. A rising crescendo of alien animal noises outside suggested the approach of morning, and the due lightening of the sky was their introduction to the first real day of the survival game.

Bogaert's first action was to complete his water still. As in other areas where the alien technology ran parallel to Terran, the *ransad* use of electricity followed from the same basic principles. However, the components and methods used were complex and strange. Having determined which output nibs were responsible for powering the emergency lighting supply, Bogaert found it necessary to abandon any ideas of using the original *ransad* circuitry, and was forced to wire in a new circuit of his own. This was complicated by the fact that he had no insulated wire, only a supply of stiff, drawn-metal thread possibly intended for making fences.

He was able to succeed with this circuit solely because the low voltage of the supply made no great demands on the quality of the insulation. Using pieces of cloth and sacking, he was able to keep the wires from shorting together. Zim covered him with the ion gun while he set up his apparatus just outside the hull. The wire proved to have the necessary resistance, and from it he was able to fashion a crude heater and secure it beneath his still in a bed of stones. The next step was to obtain some more water, with which to test the apparatus. Eying the uninviting trail that led to the swamp, Bogaert was conscious of the dangers which attended every step. Visibility and mobility were the things needed most. Starting out with Zim and several large canisters converted to water holders with long string handles, Bogaert tested the foliage for its ability to burn as it stood. Most was too moist and fleshy, but selected groups of bushes of a particularly dry texture took fire readily and burned with a heat which dried and charred some of the surrounding vegetation. Thus it was that in the course of their progress down to the swamp they considerably broadened the previous trail and gave themselves a more adequate view of potential danger. Indeed, their success was such that Bogaert determined to clear as large an area as possible as soon as time allowed.

By a combination of design and luck, the electric still worked well. They now had sufficient drinking water, but little to spare for washing—which was becoming a necessity because the rain of airborne sap droplets was continuous. The supply of wire was insufficient to build a second still, but Bogaert determined to build a sun-heated still when their more urgent problems had been overcome.

Having tested the emergency lighting with the still in operation and found no discernible drop in the voltage, Bogaert had reasoned that he had plenty of power in reserve. For this piece of good fortune he immediately found a use. The extent of their fire-raising activities on the way to the swamp had completely exhausted the fuel in his lighter. Lacking native skill in fire-making, they were now without means of making fire, although, with a short piece of the resistance wire hooked into the circuit, he could produce sufficient heat to ignite a mat of tinder. The Colonel regarded a continuing fire as a good deterrent against marauding creatures and a way of gradually clearing the undergrowth from around the barge.

The next problem was food—not obtaining it, for fruits, berries, and tubers grew in fleshy abundance, but knowing what might and might not be safe to eat. Since the flora was indigenous, all previous experience with similar-looking plants on other worlds could be discounted. Bogaert had therefore set Miram to watch carefully since the early morning to see if she could discover which plants provided food for the animals and which were avoided. Even with this information, there was still no certainty that the human stomach would be adapted to digest it, and it was a certainty that some animals would be able to tolerate vegetable poisons which humans could not. Nevertheless, it was the only way to start.

The results of Miram's observations were interesting.

Something very fleeting, with large razor-sharp horns, had disturbed an area of loam beneath a tree and eaten avidly of the white nodules it uncovered between the roots. Bogaert secured some of the nodules and tasted one with caution. It would have made a creditable ink eraser, but was tough, gritty, and utterly without taste. He boiled a few in a little of the distilled water, and they softened to a starchlike consistency with a faintly aromatic odor. There was no way of telling whether this starch paste, as they called it, had any human food value, but the cautious consumption of a small portion produced no ill effects. In the absence of any better information, they decided to include it in their diet along with boiled beans and dried nuts from the stores.

A second of Miram's observations led Bogaert to concentrate on a spiny cactuslike plant whose skin showed the ravages of many creatures small enough to penetrate between the spines. Small stem bulges, carefully peeled and quartered, yielded a sweet, pithy fruit reminiscent of melon. The sticky liquid it exuded was undoubtedly a form of sugar. They called it sugar fruit and, to prove it was acceptable to all manner of creatures, laid small portions out on leaves at the edge of the swamp track, where it was quickly eaten by a whole range of passing animals.

The finding of two apparently edible substances in such close proximity greatly improved Bogaert's views about their potential food supply. Contrary to his fears, many of the indigenous life forms seemed to have a body chemistry closely related to the galactic norm—a common occurrence on most of the inhabited star worlds. That the other contestant in the survival game was a native of the planet suggested human-utilizable food chains, which should logically include at least a proportion of the animals. The promise of meat was very welcome, but they had already achieved a subsistence diet, and the Colonel's next priority was defense rather than hunting.

It proved more difficult than he had supposed to close the rent in the *ransad* alloy hull. The curious thing about the alloy was that, although it bent, it did not become stretched in the process. When he finally managed to apply sufficient leverage to spring the torn metal back into place, it closed the gap completely, and one could detect where the tear had been only if one knew of its previous existence.

Reopening the door hatch was easier. An outrigger had split a tree during their descent, and the fragmented wood was pressed hard against the outside of the door. With an ax, he chopped away the entire tree, while Zim stood with the pistol to guard him in case of attack. The thing that impressed Bogaert was that the pod, after the enormous stresses of the crash, was still in remarkably good shape. That it had been constructed by star craftsmen working religiously according to the *ransad* texts was a tremendous tribute to the unknown compilers of the ancient manuals, both for their knowledge and for their ability to communicate.

At the end of the first day, Bogaert had taken stock of their achievements and deficiencies. They now had some known foodstufs and the promise of more. They had clean water for drinking, although not enough for bathing. They had a tolerable shelter, but were critically lacking in means of defense and knowledge of their environment. Their retention of the powerbarge and its power unit was a factor which stood greatly in their favor. Zim's gun, limited though it was, was another asset the game's designers had not foreseen—but Bogaert knew they must be wary of complacency. To relax even for a short period could be fatal.

The lesson was clear: they, like the creatures of Avida, could survive only by a continued and unremitting attack on the problems created by their environment. They would have to press every advantage to the limit, and make their own advantages where none came naturally. Only in this way could they gain a tactical reserve of time and resources which could aid them when the survival game turned its more deadly tokens.

Throughout the succeeding days, this principle of defense by attack became paramount. With Zim to cover him, Bogaert deliberately cleared a wide area around the ship, firing what was immediately combustible and chopping down that which was not. It was difficult and dangerous work. Several attacks by animals were defeated only by Zim's weapon and his hair-fine sensitivity, which enabled him to anticipate trouble shortly before it made itself manifest.

Having cleared most of the trees and brush from the immediate area, they had better access to strong sunlight. Bogaert stripped the plastic domes from a couple of the instrument cells, and made a crude sun-powered still, which provided a welcome supplement to their water supply and gave them enough for an occasional wash.

Throughout this period, Miram showed something of the mettle of which star royalty was made. Recognizing that Bogaert was both mentor and protector, she made a particular point of relieving him of as many jobs as she could. She was remarkably quick at learning, and the mantle of her upbringing dropped swiftly from her shoulders as she fought strenuously with the most menial of tasks, and even masked her revulsion at skinning and gutting the small animals which began to be caught in Bogaert's snares. Her transition from a court ornament to a tough human animal fighting for the survival of herself and her children revealed to Bogaert a little of what old Sashu had known when he had sent the trio unaccompanied from Meon.

THIRTEEN

So great was Bethschant's exhaustion after the swamp crossing that he awoke to find the sun signaling midday through the leafy cover of the great trees. He rose painfully and examined his injuries and abrasions. Most were responding adequately to the natural ability of his body to repair itself, but there were angry places on his legs which would be slow to heal unless he could find a salve. As usual on Avida, herbs suitable for the purpose were growing in close abundance. He beat the leathery leaves with a stone to bring the sap to the surface before he bound them around his legs with pieces of vine.

The raft had been almost entirely absorbed by the living slime under the bank. Bethschant viewed this disinterestedly, it being axiomatic that a new one would have to be built before the journey could continue. Because of the time needed to locate sufficient cane at exactly the right stage of maturity, he knew a couple of days must pass before he could resume his search for the Terran. This respite would also enable his skin to repair itself for the next round of assaults. Thus, his priority was to explore his immediate habitat to determine what type of camp would be most appropriate.

A swift survey of the long, narrow island assured him no large creatures inhabited it—which was logical in view of its isolated situation. All his usual enemies were there, however: sting-wings from the swamp, a multiplicity of flesh beetles, snappers, and various small carnivorous reptiles, together with fast-creepers and parasitic horrors too numerous to classify. The conclusion was that sleeping on the ground other than in very hot ash would be dangerous. His thoughts therefore turned again to the trees.

One end of the island was bare for some considerable distance; the only vegetation which existed in the area was one enormous tree of the rare non-sap variety, which had literally thrust the rocks apart to drive its roots into some deep nutrient layer. Isolated as it was from the main pool of wildlife, it naturally attracted Bethschant's attention as an outstanding prospect for a camp. Climbing it, he found it singularly uninhabited, which should have made him doubly cautious, but he was misled by regarding its isolation as the reason for its unusual lack of population.

He climbed high into the tree for a tactical investigation prior to the elaborate work of preparing it as a camp. Standing separately, the tree had grown without hindrance, and its luxuriant foliage formed a dome which would ideally contain the aromatic smoke which Bethschant would use to deter winged insects and animals. Indeed, as he climbed closer to the leafy canopy he imagined he could already smell the smoke rising from below him. Cautioning himself against any such flights of fancy, he tested the slight wind, and broke through the leaf screen at an appropriate angle to look across the intervening strip of swamp to the neighboring mainland.

He expected to see a forest fire sweeping the region. What he saw was three distinct plumes of smoke, each concentrated, as if from separate, tended fires. Here, in a situation mainly above the arboreal ceiling, the forest sounds came through with unnatural clarity. Bethschant was still pondering on the unlikely circumstance of three distinct fires when his ears detected what could only be the sound of an ax striking wood. The distance was such that he could easily have been mistaken, but with his hearing and perception suddenly attuned, he now heard the sound repeated at regular intervals. The conclusion was inescapable: the Terran was not only alive but actually engaged in making a clearing in the forest.

The surprise of the discovery left Bethschant trembling. Whereas he had thought himself alone on the whole planet, here was clear evidence of someone else living and in good health, to judge by the frequency and regularity of the ax blows. Although the man was an enemy and would have to be killed, Bethschant was suddenly glad Colonel Bogey had managed to survive. He felt a sudden kinship with this other human, and a great relief as the weight of his own absolute loneliness was lifted from his scarred shoulders.

His objective changed imperceptibly. More than wanting to kill the Terran, he first wanted to look at him. He needed to hear the sound of a human voice in the Avidan forest, to have actual sight of another human being moving over Avida's deadly and too-fertile land. He stayed over-long clinging to his precarious perch, straining all his senses to try to catch a fragment more evidence of this incredible survival. The further sound he did hear filled him with an unholy joy and purpose. Above the forest murmur had come the clear and distant call of an unmistakably female voice.

"Bogey! Bogey!"

The sound ricocheted around Bethschant's brain. A woman on Avida? The idea was impossible, yet he had the evidence of his senses. Her voice was not that of one of the apelike females of Avidan stock, like his own erstwhile mate. Here was an outworld woman, perhaps one of those creamy, desirable females from the star worlds whose attractions had caused Bethschant so much trouble during his service with Xzan. This, Bethschant reasoned, was the answer to all his most impious prayers. Certainly Colonel Bogey would have to be killed—but Bethschant could think of a thousand better things he could do with a star woman on this planet, where he and the Avidan gods were the only arbiters of events.

His preoccupation with lecherous daydreams kept Bethschant in the tree for most of the remaining day. Hunger finally drove him down from his perch. It was the wrong time of day to hunt small game. He therefore contented himself with fruits and canenuts before reluctantly returning to the preparations for night defense.

His expertise at fire-making failed him time after time. It was very nearly dark before he had the aromatic smoke winding up through the high branches. The loss of light robbed him of the opportunity to encircle the bole with rawthorns or cut the fast-creeper which draped itself casually on the underside of the great boughs. He spent the remaining moments of twilight scraping the bark from the branches on which he intended to sleep. He admitted to himself that he was not properly prepared for the night, but in times of fatigue or illness he had taken greater risks than this and still survived.

His sense of oneness with Avida was disturbed during the night by a series of broken and erotic dreams which were neither satisfying nor conducive to the freedom from movement necessary in one sleeping in the branches of a tree. As it was, the fitful nature of his sleep probably saved his life. The gentle pressures across his groin, which in sleep he had associated with the softness of human flesh, remained as a cold, vegetable hardness when he awoke. Striving to move, he found a similar loop encompassing his chest. His alerted senses immediately warned him that he was being attacked by a fast-creeper, and that only minutes remained before the intelligent vine managed to encircle him so many times that he would lose all power to move his limbs.

In the darkness, his hand caught an exploring tip-bud. He chopped at it with the side of his palm, hoping to snap the stem. The resilience of the vine, however, enabled it to avoid damage. Although it withdrew, he knew it was only to describe a wider arc before it wrapped around his shoulders or his neck. His fingers thankfully reached the handle of his long-knife. Although his arms were pinioned against his chest, he managed to hack at the branch beneath him, trying to strike a point where it was intersected by the fast-creeper. For a long time this awkward action met with no success. Finally he felt the pressure across his groin begin to slacken, and then he was able to bend the coil around his chest and arrive at a sitting position.

The situation was worse than he had feared. While he had slept, festoons of fast-creeper had risen from the lower branches to attack him from all sides. Had he not awakened when he did, it must certainly have immobilized and devoured him. However, it was no match for a long-knife, and he had soon scythed away a whole host of fleshy, inquisitive tip-buds and severed every flying trunk or streamer which wavered within arm's length.

Trembling with reaction at the narrowness of his escape, Bethschant knew he would have to move away from the immediate area, because the plant knew his location and would continue to attack that part while it had any mobile appendages left. Escape was not easy. Tree-climbing in absolute darkness was very dangerous, and the most he dared do was make his way along the branch on which he had been sleeping, down to a crevice it formed with the main trunk of the tree. There he wedged himself to wait for the coming of daylight.

While he was thus occupied, he heard below something he could scarcely have conceived in his worst nightmares. This was a constant chattering noise as made by armor-clad snappers, whose ferocity was legend. The sound was not isolated; it was repeated as though multiplied by countless hundreds. Sickly, Bethschant realized into what circumstance he had led himself. The barrenness of the rocks beneath the tree took on a morbid significance. Below the rocks must be a major snapper colony, and the surrounding area would have been thoroughly scavenged by the young from the nests, even though the adults traveled far in their remorseless search for flesh.

He questioned himself sternly about how he had come to make so grave a mistake. The answer was that he had been careless. Snappers were usually but not invariably nocturnal. He had arrived at the tree and made preparations for the night at a time when the whole snapper colony was undergoing a major sleep period. Perhaps his fire or the noise he had made fighting the creeper had disturbed them. Now the whole colony encircled the tree, and, from what he knew of their patience and determination, they were unlikely to go away while such a tempting flesh morsel hung above their heads.

Snappers could not climb, but their agility was such that they could jump several man-heights, and their reaction speed made one fully a match for a seasoned warrior. To descend into their midst was unthinkable, and there were no other trees through which he might escape. While he crouched, uncomfortable and afraid, the gradual light of dawn began to fill in the visual details of what his imagination had already told him was the terrible truth.

The growing light also showed something which gave him a glimmer of hope. No snappers dared approach the slow fire that even now drifted its long streamers of vapor into the air. His weapon against so many snappers could only be fire, and if he could make fire in the tree and drop it down on them, he would stand a chance of gaining an escape route. The chances of finding sufficient flammable material up a tree seemed unlikely, but the unlikely proved possible once he had decided what needed to be done. Generations of fast-creeper had populated the boughs, died, and withered, leaving great festoons of dried vine hanging from the branches. Had the tree been of the acid-sap variety, these remnants would have been digested and fallen as powder, but in this particular tree the loops still clung dryly to the branches they had hugged in life.

He started collecting dead vines, intending to light fires at various points on the branches, from which he could drop the flaming masses. After he lit one fire, however, the flames spread with an astonishing rapidity along the overhanging loops of creeper, and soon the sparks and tongues of flame had made their own way throughout the entire interior vastness of the tree. The result was far better than he could have anticipated. Burning streamers dropped from all sides like incandescent rain. The panic among the snappers manifested itself in an untidy, angry exodus, which took them not along the island, as Bethschant had expected, but leaping and floundering out across the swamp tracts in the direction of the mainland.

Suddenly Bethschant understood why the snappers were so numerous in an area which could not have supported them all. From the island to the mainland there must be a slightly submerged causeway across which the snappers could gain access to the larger territory. The place he had disturbed was probably only a breeding nest, and all the regular foraging would be done on the other side of the swamp.

His further consideration of the point was cut short by the requirements of his own safety. Not only had most of the creeper burned, but now part of the host tree was also catching fire. Super-heated sap sprouted long jets of flame, which further increased the conflagration. By the time he reached the ground, the radiant heat had already become unbearable, and he had to pick his way carefully through the masses of live embers lest he severly burn his feet. His final consolation was to pick up a couple of partly roasted snappers, whose cooking he then proceeded to complete. It had been a long time since he had tasted roast snapper for breakfast.

FOURTEEN

Trouble came early. Zim, who had gone confidently out to examine snares, came back hastily with the information that a whole legion of crab-rats was advancing from the direction of the swamp. His suggestion of an army was no less than the truth. By midday, many hundreds of the fearsome creatures had moved into the area and were sunning themselves in the open spaces Bogaert and Zim had so laboriously cleared.

It was impossible for the occupants of the pod to consider driving them off. Any single creature was fully a match for an armed man, and the horrific tide surrounded the ship completely. Effectively, the humans were besieged, with access to neither food nor water. Some of the crab-rats were even investigating the nearby rocky outcrop, as if considering the site for a nest. A large group waited impatiently close to the pod, attracted by the scent of human flesh inside.

Occasionally, Zim opened the door hatch and fired at the creatures with his ion gun. He killed a few and wounded many, but even the wounded returned and waited expectantly for the door to open wider. Zim could not hope to shoot many with his malfunctioning weapon, and it would be far too dangerous to attempt to carry on the fight with other weapons.

Through a viewing port, Bogaert noted that the crab-rats that crossed the bare wires leading to the still leaped away as though receiving an unwelcome shock. He decided that an electrical attack on the creatures might succeed if he could somehow increase the voltage. On each of the preceding days, he had spent an hour working on the power plant, trying to restore its output above the existing trickle level. Given access to a workshop, he could probably have regained full power in a matter of days. As it was, he had a dangerous and tricky job, applying makeshift levers against truly amazing forces. Spurred by this new necessity, he tackled the reluctant unit with an urgency that made little concession to the very considerable risk of losing a finger or a hand should his precarious system of stops and levers collapse under the opposing forces.

His Herculean efforts were rewarded when he managed to achieve a gap between the output plates into which he could slip an Ortellian wedge-hammer. As he did so, the metal bar he had been using as a lever fractured without warning. The broken metal spun across the cabin, hitting the back of his wrist as it did so. Fortunately, it was only a glancing blow which did no more than raise an ominous bruise. It could as easily have broken his wrist.

Testing the output, he found he now had the equivalent of one hundred twenty-seven Terran volts. This was only half of what he felt he needed, but time was running out, and hopefully even this would be sufficient to stun or kill a crab-rat.

He already had two bare wires rigged outside the hull to power the electric still. If he now applied the full available voltage to these, he would burn out his precious heater and destroy their main source of pure water. He therefore connected the supply to only one of these wires, and the other he affixed directly to the hull. He was confident that the construction of the still would afford a ground connection, but there was an anxious moment as he brought the voltage up to full value, because he had no way of testing the pod's own electrical contact with the ground. Fortunately, only a negligible current flowed, indicating that the barge was reasonably well insulated by the ceramic tips of the outriggers.

Being themselves inside the electrically charged pod, they were not affected, and they gathered close to the viewing ports to watch the results outside. Whenever a crab-rat touched the hull, it gave a truly amazing jump into the air and fell either dead or stunned some considerable distance away. There appeared to be an element of learning involved, and the mistake was repeated by only a few crab-rats before the lesson was learned. Bogaert decided it was time to carry the fight into the open.

The instrument he decided to use was adapted from a rakelike tool with a long cane stem. By attaching one end of the wire to the tines and the other to the charged hull of the pod, he produced an electrified weapon which he could safely hold by the cane-insulated handle. Warning Zim, who insisted on following, to jump clear of the hull and not to touch both it and the ground simultaneously, Bogaert emerged from the door hatch and began his assault.

The crab-rats had been waiting for just such an opportunity, and swarmed around for the kill. The combined effects of accidental contact with the hull and the Colonel's sterling work with the electrified rake soon caused them to change their minds. Their vicious swarming became an uncontrolled rout as inert bodies piled up before this unfamiliar and deadly enemy. Such was the communal sense of the creatures that at some signal undetectable by human senses, virtually the whole of the survivors—probably only half the original colony—turned as if impelled by a single command and fled into the forest cover.

Bogaert surveyed the retreat with much relief, and was about to reenter the pod when a shout of warning from Zim made him freeze. Three of the creatures had leaped onto an outrigger, from which, having no contact with the ground, they could move without danger of electrocution. They were about to launch themselves at his neck and back, an act which must certainly prove fatal to him, when Zim's single shot vaporized one in mid-flight and so disconcerted the others that they missed the target completely. On instinct, Bogaert used the rake not for electrocution but in the manner of a club, striking the bodies with a strong swing. One was electrocuted; the other was lifted bodily and hurled almost to the limits of the clearing.

Things grew quieter then, although the creatures could still be seen lingering on the fringes of the clearing. Bogaert decided the time was ripe to improve on his advantage. He staked out a wide area around the stricken ship and ran a bare wire around it, which he then electrified. It was a hasty, makeshift job, but it promised to keep the foraging crab-rats at bay until a better defense could be constructed.

Miram, whose eye for edible substances was becoming delicately practiced, considered that crab-rats should make good eating. They picked a few prize specimens from among the newly dead, and began to clean the carcasses. This involved splitting the armored shells, in the course of which Miram cut her hand badly. Bogaert was worried as he washed the wound, knowing the grave risk of infection. His concern, and the increased power available from the power plant, made him decide immediately to try another device he had in mind.

He had been collecting the concentrated brine sludge from the stills, and had successfully purified some by recrystallization. Some of this rock salt had been crushed for cooking, and all of the remainder he now redissolved in an apparatus he hastily constructed from some pottery utensils and some pieces of carbon broken out of a *ransad* cell.

Zim watched the improvisation with considerable interest.

"What're we making, Bogey?"

"We need some antiseptic for your mother's hand. We're trying to break down the salt using electricity to give us two chemicals called sodium hydroxide and chlorine. If we can get them to react together, we'll form another chemical, called sodium hypochlorite. That's the one we're after. It makes a good antiseptic."

The first results were not encouraging, but, by pressing both Zim and Arma into service, pouring the liquid repeatedly through the assembly, Bogaert finally produced a result he decided by taste and smell was as near as he was likely to get to the desired composition. He tried some on his own scratched arms. The stinging was considerable, and the remedial effects not obvious, but the mixture, whatever its composition, was the nearest to an antiseptic preparation they were likely to obtain.

He diluted some with some pure water and took a jar of it to Miram. She was in the pod, trying to continue the preparation of the food using only one hand, and not making a very good job of it. She allowed him to recleanse and dress the wound, even though the stinging brought tears to her eyes. When it was finished and neatly dressed with strips of torn cloth, she reached out with her good hand and grasped his wrist as a sign of gratitude. The sensation of her fingers fired a spark in his consciousness, which shook him nearly as much as the electrical shocks had shaken the crab-rats. He recovered from his mental somersault vividly aware that although this was the first time they had been alone together, there were some very good reasons why it should also be the last.

The crab-rat meat proved superb. Roasted on a spit turned by the dogged little Arma, it was tender and succulent. Unfortunately, they were unable to preserve any of their present surfeit. Regretfully, Zim and Bogaert shoveled away the remaining carcasses to a position under one of the great trees, where the enzyme sap would rapidly destroy and digest the remains with the accelerated rotting which was part of the life cycle of the forest.

The same sap was, at this time, causing other problems. Clothing materials of natural origin had begun to fall apart, and even some of the synthetic fibers were affected. Bogaert had felled most of the closest trees, but the slight drift of the aerosol out of the forest still brought enough enzyme to promote the destruction of most of their garments. Miram's propriety was maintained only by frequent changes of clothes with which she had been provided by Manu Kan. Zim was enjoying the previously forbidden luxury of going about nearly naked, while Arma was fortunate in having almost the only garment which was impervious to the attack. Bogaert's uniform was in shreds, and made him look like a military scarecrow.

Not only their clothing was suffering. Their hair, too, became brittle and broke off close to the scalp. The psychological effect was reduced by it being a gradual process rather than a sudden loss, and new hair continued to grow healthily at the roots. Bogaert accepted the consequent close-cropped effect with stoicism. It changed his appearance very little. Miram, whose honey-gray tresses had been a cherished possession, was horrified until she accepted that it probably enhanced her new image as a practical savage, and underscored the strengths she found growing in herself.

All the rest of the day the crab-rats remained at the fringes of the forest. The few which strayed as far as Bogaert's fence died, apparently as object lessons for the others.

After their evening meal, Zim and the Colonel checked the wire, and found to their concern that a great many of the cane supports were already beginning to crumble. This was remarkable, because the canes had appeared perfectly sound when put into place a few hours earlier. Apparently this type of cane was very susceptible to the acid sap, and the supports close to the forest edge were already critically decayed. They carefully replaced those they found to be defective, but had doubts about the remainder lasting through the night.

Toward evening, the crab-rats began to move back closer to the wire. With them now were a great number of smaller crab-rats who had not been apparent in the earlier fray. Miram decided that these must be the young of the species, and that the whole colony had probably had to abandon a previous breeding ground and was now looking for another. Bogaert's worry was that the electrified fence, supported as it was on unreliable cane, would fail during the night and allow the creatures to repeat their attack.

The recent clearing activities had left them with an ample supply of dry brushwood. The Colonel took the precaution of lighting a number of fires around the perimeter as an additional deterrent. To speed this task before darkness, the others came to assist. Thus it was that they all happened to be away from the ship and at the far end of the clearing when disaster struck.

Whether it was a short circuit or a break in the wire was not apparent. Arma's startled cry signaled the fact that crab-rats by the hundreds were now crossing over or under the wire with impunity, and that the majority of them were running straight for the open door of the pod. Several of the larger ones, however, broke away and turned toward the end of the clearing where the horrified humans were tending their fires.

The first of the crab-rats to approach was dropped by a burst from Zim's ion gun—which was then useless for the ten minutes it took to recharge. Ten seconds would have been too long a delay. Bogaert played the only move available. Seizing burning branches with his bare hands, he dragged two fires together and made a flaming wall between them and the attacking creatures. He immediately did the same with two more adjacent fires, so that he achieved a horseshoe of flame around them.

The effect was dramatic. The crab-rats made a cursory attempt to find a way through, failed to find the open end of the horseshoe, then retired to join their fellows in the rush for the pod. The night became complete, with only the Hub stars and the light from the fires for illumination, but from what little could be seen, it was certain that the crab-rats had adopted the pod as a new and novel kind of nest.

The loss of their major asset in the fight for survival filled Bogaert with apprehension. He realized, even if the others did not, that they were unlikely to survive many days without the shelter and facilities the power-barge made available. The question was how to regain the pod from such a concentration of ferocious and deadly foes. Any attempt at entry would be impossible, and even if he managed to find a way to drive them out, they would still be at liberty to menace the district. The best solution would be to kill them in the pod, but the means by which this could be done were not immediately apparent. After some thought, the Colonel and

Zim left the women safely behind a circle of fires and, each carrying a burning brand, advanced carefully toward the ship.

Apparently the crab-rat colony did not consider it necessary to guard their new nest. The two men approached warily without meeting any sign of roving creatures. Their first action was to insert a piece of branch in the hatch frame and slam and prop the door so that it was almost but not entirely closed. This action raised a great tide of animal movement within the ship, but Bogaert had judged the width of the gap to a nicety. None of the claws which appeared at the gap could reach them as they further secured a rope around the hull to reinforce the prop.

Breathing a sigh of relief at the ease of the creatures' containment, Bogaert used the light of a burning brand to examine the apparatus he had used for making the antiseptic. Although the high-voltage wire around the clearing had failed, the lower-voltage line connected to the carbon electrodes in the salt solution was still functioning. He lifted the top off the aparatus and carried the pieces to the door hatch. There he made a crude modification, which he then sealed against the gap in the door with the remains of his uniform jacket trapped beneath a loop of rope.

"And that's all we can do," he said to Zim. "I've taken the top off the pot so the chlorine gas can escape. A lot of it'll go through the gap into the pod. With luck, it'll poison our friends inside."

"Is it very poisonous?"

"Very. It's a nasty way to kill, but I don't have any option. We need the pod back—and we need it fast. It's them or us."

"How long will the chlorine take?"

"There's no way of knowing. Certainly we don't dare open it before morning, perhaps not even then. But it's better than losing the pod altogether. Let's get back to the fires, because I think we're going to have a very hard night."

FIFTEEN

The Pretender's continued presence in the quaint and ornate halls of Oontara's court was motivated by nothing stronger than clutching at straws. While all the evidence pointed to Miram's having taken her children to Terra, Camin Sher conducted a frantic search for anything which suggested they might actually have gone somewhere more accessible. Behind his standpoint was the knowledge that Kanizar had no treaty with Terra; therefore, the destination was unlikely as a refuge for his wife and heirs. He suspected that the mention of Terra was part of a trick to throw him off the scent. If the Empress had indeed reached such inviolable territory, however, Sher had damned himself without gain. His attack on Meon could be justified only by the assassination of Kanizar's hereditary successors. If he failed in this, all his other victories were a mere prelude to his final defeat at Kanizar's vengeful hands.

The immoderate sums of money he had to pay for the records of the shipping agency which handled Terran space transportation was a reminder to Sher that he was operating in a region where he was not recognized as a potential king of kings. Instead, he was treated with the offhand disrespect merited by a potential loser. Nonetheless, the records appeared to prove that the rendezvous with the Terra-bound starliner had indeed been arranged. They further showed that a second pickup had been arranged for the same outspace rendezvous. This duplication held no immediate significance for the Pretender, since in neither case had a passenger list been filed.

His first piece of luck came with the location of a spacegram from the captain of the spaceliner berating the shipping agency for causing him to break out of hyperspace for a rendezvous which had not been kept. Camin Sher's next thoughts were to locate the vessel which had been engaged to make the rendezvous. The search narrowed down to one possible barge, which was the subject of ghost control by a father ship. The father ship had long since left the system, but was speedily traced through the cargo lists. Since it was operating a returning shuttle service, units of Camin Sher's fleet were despatched to intercept the Master. They reported that the Master denied all knowledge of the incident and neither bribery nor threats could make him move from this position.

On the rising hope that Miram had not reached Terra, Sher refused to let the matter rest. He sent again for Xzan and set the facts before him. Xzan queried the details meticulously, then with growing delight he turned back to the Pretender.

"My Lord knows my desire to serve him faithfully. I think I can show proof of my intent."

"Stop planting words and come to the point," Sher answered acidly. "If you've anything relevant, tell it now before Kanizar destroys us all."

"I've no facts to go on, you'll understand. But the circumstance of the barge and the unkept rendezvous are familiar. Oontara and I'd wagered on a survival game. My champion was willing, but Oontara's had to be 'acquired.' The barge and the false rendezvous was the ruse by which we secured the Terran Colonel Bogey for the sport."

"What has this to do with the Kanizars?"

"We forced a diversion of a barge intended to make rendezvous with the starliner. It's unlikely there were two barges similarly engaged that evening."

"You mean . . . ?"

"From the evidence you've given me, there's a more than adequate chance that our net caught also Kanizar's woman and the Kanizar spawn. They've all been included in our survival game. They're probably dead already."

"I'll need evidence of that." Sher's hopes were on a flowing tide. "Where'd you put them, Xzan?"

"My Lord will remember I'm not yet a king—"

"I'll make you a king. Tell me where."

"Not that I expect rewards out of proportion to the service—"

"Ten times a king," said Sher hastily. "What's the location?"

"Avida. One of the subtler hells."

"I don't want a travelogue. I want star references."

Xzan found them for him, wondering what being ten times a king might feel like.

Camin Sher's reaction was immediate. Without a further glance at the beaming Xzan, he called for his aides, then left the court at a pace which gave every indication of his urgency. On the way down the corridor, the hurrying group passed a small, balding figure dressed in crumpled white, who raised an eyebrow in silent speculation.

As the Pretender hurried out of sight, Hilary Rounding wandered into the room they had just vacated and slapped Star Lord Xzan heartily across the shoulders.

"My Lord looks pleased yet quizzical. Could it be he's as puzzled as I about the speed of the Pretender's departure?"

Xzan's eyes were still fixed on the doorway through which the Pretender had run. "Not at all. But I wonder if he'll remember who told him where to go."

"I've much difficulty in understanding the motivations of the great star monarchs," said the dumpling sadly, examining a set of shipping-agency records and a star gazeteer which were open on the table.

"I don't have trouble with their motivations," said Xzan. "It's keeping them to their promises I find difficult. Sometimes I think I'd have been better advised to remain with Kanizar."

"Is the Pretender's rescue mission associated with the missing Kanizars, then?"

"Rescue mission?" Xzan regarded his inquisitor with dismay. "I forgot. You're a Terran. You can't be expected to understand the complexities of star politics."

"I'm afraid you're right there," said Rounding humbly. "I'm naive and incurably romantic. You know, I even like every story to have a happy ending."

"The truth of this story'd make your hair stand on end." Xzan found himself staring fixedly at Rounding's bald pate, slightly embarrassed to realize how inappropriate his metaphor had been. Then he looked accusingly into Rounding's eyes, as if he had just become aware of his presence for the first time. "You know, I think you're trying to pump me, Commissioner. But I've nothing to say."

"Perish the thought!" said Rounding, departing the scene with a star gazeteer, page-marked by the insertion of a folded spacegram, draped casually under his arm.

If Xzan's feelings were already slightly mixed, they were completely scrambled by the imperious summons he received from Oontara.

"I've my explanations," said the star king, "as to why the Pretender came to Ortel. I leave it to you to explain why he left so hurriedly."

Xzan tried to be placating. "It's something you'd scarcely believe, old friend. A coincidence beyond belief."

"Try it on me," said Oontara. "My powers of credulity grow with every hour of our acquaintanceship."

"The trap we set for Colonel Bogey caught other rodents as well. None less than the Empress Miram and the Kanizar heirs."

"What! And you told this to the Pretender? Did you also tell where the game world was located?"

"I mentioned the fact. There's no harm in it. The Pretender cares nothing about Colonel Bogey, and only Kanizar will have a loss to suffer."

"Then think again, star weasel. The loss will be yours also. Assuming they've survived, Colonel Bogey's unlikely to surrender a woman and two children to Sher's murdering hands. They'll have to kill him as well. Which means you lose the game by default. You'll owe me ten planets and surrender the rest of your holdings to the Federation. That was the terms of our agreement."

"But I—"

"Not that I'm complaining about that," said Oontara. "I've much to gain from it. But that's only part of the upset your idiot ego may have caused. There's a major concentration of hyperspace trails rocking the continuum. My guess is this heralds Kanizar's return. The Pretender may have the advantage in craft and guile, but if Kanizar devotes all his resources to destroying him, then the Pretender stands no chance at all. And what do you suppose the King of Kings will do to those who included his family in a survival game?"

Xzan's attempt to answer was interrupted by an apologetic servant.

"My Lord Oontara, a million pardons, but Commissioner Rounding seeks an immediate audience."

"Have him wait an hour," said Oontara. "Then I'll see him. As for Lord Xzan, see that he has every assistance in reaching his ship. I fear he has an urgent mission to perform."

SIXTEEN

The night spent in the ring of fire was the worst they had ever experienced. It confirmed Bogaert's suspicions that without the barge and its power plant, there was virtually no chance that they could have survived this far. Even in the protective circle of flame they were not immune from attack by flying creatures. All the quartet received painful multiple stings from smaller flying species, but mercifully avoided some of the larger winged horrors, the size of Terran bats, which were probably capable of giving a fatal injection.

There were also flying things with teeth and claws. They all now carried branches, with which they attempted to knock these flying beasts down into the flames, and each guarded the others in case something slipped through unnoticed. Such unceasing vigilance permitted no sleep, and would lead all four of them to complete exhaustion if they did not regain the pod in a couple of days. In any case, sleeping on the ground was out of the question. The flesh-seeking fibers grew a centimeter a minute from the ground wherever a foot was rested over-long. Such was the appetite of this life form that it literally stripped the skin from their ankles and found its way through the cracks in their rotting footwear.

Even though there were no trees overhead, the drift of enzyme sap seemed even more vehement. It glazed their skins where it dried in the heat from the fire, making them feel even more wretched than before. The night noises, too, crowded in on them with screams of abject terror and outbursts of hysterical laughter. Somewhere out in the swamp something called in an unbelievably human voice. The Colonel thought it called, "Bogey! Bogey! Bogey!" but Miram was certain it was calling her. The children heard it with mortal apprehension, but refused to name their fears.

Bogaert blessed his foresight in clearing the area of brush. This had encouraged many of the larger creatures to move away and so not contribute to the present danger. Even so, he could see some particularly venomous-looking articulated sticks slithering not far beyond the fires. Occasionally some gross animal head, warty and toothed or fanged, would loom up with hungry eyes, mournfully seeking a route to the human party. None had yet dared attempt to leap the flames, and the tired Zim had been able to reserve the shot in his ion gun for a really prime emergency.

Dawn was one of the most welcome sights they had ever known. With the growing light, the attack of the insects abated. A fine rain saturated the air, a solace indeed to their smoke-dried and sap-glazed skin. The interlude gave Bogaert the chance to move more cut brush into the vicinity, so that the fires could be continued if required. Then, when the light had grown sufficient to see details at a distance, he and Zim went warily toward the ship to assess the results of their move against the crab-rats.

When they could see the door hatch clearly, they stopped in disbelief. The chlorine generator had been knocked on its side, and the rope securing the door had been cut or broken. The door stood open wide enough to have permitted the escape of any crab-rat that had cared to leave. Bogaert's jacket, used to guide the gas into the door gap now lay many meters away.

Their immediate fear was that the crab-rats had managed to escape, and knocked over the chlorine generator in their flight. Bogaert and Zim turned anxiously to scan the forest fringes. The scene, however, remained curiously quiet.

Their suspicions unconfirmed, the two approached the pod with utmost caution, being constantly prepared to run for their lives. The rope had been severed cleanly, as if by a sharp knife. With a long stick, Bogaert cautiously levered open the door hatch. Something moved very swiftly through the gap—but it was only a dead crab-rat falling out. Recovering from the shock, they moved back again and opened the door wide enough to see inside. The pod was stacked high with dead crab-rats, literally hundreds of them, now fallen in strained heaps and piles between the clamps of stores. Each was twisted in the agonies of painful death.

Breathing a sigh of relief, Bogaert propped the door wide open. It would take many hours before the gas inside would disperse sufficiently to make it safe to reclaim their shelter. He sent Zim to advise the women of the situation, and turned his attention to trying to decide who or what could have cut the rope and allowed the door to open. Hilary Rounding had suggested that another contestant was to be placed on Avida. The Commissioner had also been convinced that the game would be loaded against the Terran. Putting these things together, the Colonel came up with a reasonable conjecture as to the identity of their mysterious visitor, if not the motive which had brought him so stealthily through the night.

Bogaert tried to imagine the nocturnal visitor's surprise when he had attempted to enter the pod. It was difficult to say whether the effect of finding it full of crab-rats would have been more or less daunting than finding it full of concentrated chlorine gas. Certainly it was an experiment which would be repeated only with great caution. The fact that it might be repeated, however, was itself a cause for concern.

It was Zim who found evidence of the correctness of Bogaert's assumptions regarding the opening of the pod. On his way back with Miram and Arma, he had found a long-knife dropped among the ferns. Searching around, he found five short spears, all made from local cane and tipped with obsidian shards dipped in what he presumed to be poison. It appeared that all of these items had been dropped in the course of a headlong flight from the pod. Bogaert guessed that the intruder had unsuspectingly taken a lungful of chlorine, and fled in extreme pain. It was not clear whether the visitor had known of their presence amid the fires at the end of the clearing, but he had walked into a situation as dangerous as a prepared trap. Bogaert decided the next trap would be deliberately set.

A slight breeze cleared the air in the pod rapidly, although the smell of chlorine persisted. By mid-afternoon they were able to enter and shovel the dead crab-rats to a place beneath the trees where they could safely decompose. The manner in which the creatures had died suggested the meat would be tainted, and none were saved for food.

As soon as he had a clear route to the control cabin, Bogaert left the others to continue the clearance and started work again on the power plant. Now that the reactive plates were fairly well apart, he had more room in which to manipulate his tools. He was aided by finding a strong clamp, which he used as a jack, gaining considerable mechanical advantage. After two hours of struggle, the maximum voltage available had been improved to the equivalent of nearly five hundred Terran volts, and many of the *ransad* instruments were coming back to life.

Insulation of his temporary wiring at this higher voltage was a major problem. He managed to bead the wire where it ran down through the pod with lengths of hollow cane further wrapped in pieces of packing materials. He extended two circuits—one to lethally electrify the hull, and the second to feed the loop he was intending to reconstruct as a perimeter fence round the clearing.

Curiously, the finding of the spears was of assistance in the erection of the new electrified fence. The previous fence had failed because the canes on which the wire had been suspended had rapidly rotted and allowed the conductor to short-circuit to the ground. The stem used for the spears, however, showed no sign of such deterioration. They were able to identify it as a type which grew widely on one edge of the swamp. The new fence, when completed, had two strands of wire: one set low enough to kill a crab-rat or similar small creature, and one set high enough to kill a man.

The whole system was improvised and dangerous. Miram and Arma in particular had to be instructed not to stray too close to the electrified strands or to leave the pod until they were sure the circuit had been disconnected. They had much trouble due to the antics of a peculiarly fast-growing creeper that seemed to exercise almost human ingenuity in trying to invade their territory. It was deterred by repeatedly chopping off the leading buds until it appeared to finally accept the lesson and declined to grow any farther than the fence. In the meantime, the electrocution of a number of small animals provided a steady source of meat for Miram's pot.

So passive a defense, however, was not enough for Bogaert. The presence of another human worried him even more than some of the terrifying creatures which occasionally appeared at the clearing's edge. He judged that outside the pod they were easily within range of a well-thrown spear. He took it as axiomatic that the other human was of bad intent. Life held too many hazards to take chances.

His priority thus became the improvisation of weapons and the clearance of the forest cover over a wider area by firing the trees and brush. In this latter enterprise he was initially unsuccessful. When he did manage to establish a good blaze, however, it became a major forest fire, and scarred a strip of land several kilometers in length. It was halted only by a series of muddy rivulets which stood across its path and acted as a firebreak. The clearance brought a welcome reduction in insect swarms, but meant that the traps and snares had to be set over a wider area, and fruits had to be fetched from a distance. The greater visibility afforded by the scheme, however, justified the hardships. By day they were relatively immune from surprise attacks, and by night the electrified defenses gave them a very high order of protection.

SEVENTEEN

As he entered the audience chamber, Rounding's face was more stern than Oontara remembered ever having seen it. The Terran offered no handshake and refused to take wine or a chair.

"My Lord Oontara disappoints me. I'd hoped that in embracing federation you'd also learned that human lives are not for sale or gaming."

"I won't pretend I don't know what you mean," said the star king slowly. "I know you too well. Your information's always immaculate. You're referring to Colonel Bogey."

"I am."

"You Terrans are devils. You expect too much of us. Our star customs go back to well before your own Neanderthal. You'll not reform us overnight."

"I can have a damn good try," said Rounding ominously. "I want some straight answers."

"Unless I misread you, Commissioner, you already

have your answers. You have some other point that needs making."

"The Empress Miram and her children were on the barge that took Colonel Bogey to Avida. Right or wrong?"

"Probable."

"And the Pretender's gone to arrange their assassination?"

"That too seems probable."

"Then tell me why Lord Xzan made blastoff while you had me waiting in the antechamber."

"I reminded Xzan that if the Pretender kills Colonel Bogey while attacking the Kanizars, he forfeits the game."

"And if the Kanizars are murdered without the death of Bogey, how's the situation altered?"

Oontara smiled slyly. "Then my offense against Terra is a purely technical one. And Kanizar's quarrel with me will be the slightest. After all, I didn't knowingly send Miram to Avida. Officially she was never even on Ortel. And I'll be many parsecs away when Xzan and the Pretender conspire to her murder. A rather neat piece of politics, don't you think, Commissioner?"

"That wasn't the phrase I had in mind," said Rounding savagely. "One day I'll introduce you to another aspect of the new logic—known as ethics. How the hell do you expect Xzan to stop the Pretender from killing Bogey?"

"I didn't say I could expect it. But if the crime's committed, at least the blood's not on my hands. I've done what I can without becoming further implicated."

"You've not done a tenth enough. Believe me, if Bogey's killed I'll personally make sure Kanizar has full knowledge of your part in this."

"I'd thought we were friends." Oontara's tone was faintly plaintive.

"You consistently miss the point of friendship. The point is not to appear innocent of the crime, but to prevent it from happening. The chances are Bogey and the Kanizars are still alive. I've radioed a taskforce out from Terra, but I doubt they'll reach Avida in time. But there's the possibility that they could be reached by a ship moving in from the Hub."

"You're not asking *me* to send a fleet against the Pretender?" Oontara was suddenly anxious.

"Nothing half as heroic—though I hope the idea sits heavily on your conscience. It looks as though I'll have to sort out this mess myself. But I've only workships here, and they're not fast enough."

"You'd like to borrow a star cruiser?"

"Not to put too fine an edge on it, this mission calls for characteristics which can't be found in a *ransad*-based ship. I'd like to borrow the Terran bark."

"My pleasure, Commissioner! Xzan thinks it nothing but a quaint toy."

"Then it'll please me to demonstrate otherwise."

"And you'll remember the gesture when you speak to Kanizar?"

"I'll remember it *as* a gesture. Even star kings aren't above responsibility for their own actions."

"Did nobody ever tell you you've the makings of a tyrant? By the gods, I think you'd outmaneuver Kanizar himself!"

"Possibly. But that's not the Terran way. We meet force with force, guile with guile, and honesty with honesty. It's part of the new logic: do unto others as they'd do unto you—but do it first and do it better. Have I made myself plain?"

"Crystal clear. You're a rogue without peer—and all the more dangerous because you're that curse of the galaxy, a man dedicated to furthering things other than himself."

"Amen to that!" said Hilary Rounding.

Of all the impressive man-made sights in the universe, none could compare with the massed fleets of Kanizar dropping out of hyperspace. First a solitary spacefinder would apparently materialize in space with an inaudible boom that sent a shiver through the continuum. Alone, it would sit a hundred million miles from the sun, a shining glory to those who had the instruments to see it. Then sixteen other ships would appear around it in careful station, to form a circle as large as Terra's moon.

When these markers were in position, the rest of the fleet would appear, gradually filling the interstices of the disk. Those who did not appreciate the realities of scale soon found it unbelievable that the design could continue to fill and thicken with the golden splints, each of which was a great warship with a complement of several thousand men. The ships' arrivals were timed microseconds apart, so that each sent only an ascending thrill through the continuum. Had they arrived simultaneously, the shock would have been such that the physical constants for several kilo-parsecs would have been hideously distorted and the delicate structure of spacetime ruptured for centuries. Men had been driven mad and stars turned nova by lesser assemblies than this.

Even so, the rapidity with which the great circle became a golden shield was indicative of the great urgency of the occasion. Risking the enmity of natural philosophers for generations, Kanizar had cut the emergence of his fleets from hyperspace to the finest limits safety would allow. The resonance set up in the continuum forced a thrill through every sentient creature in that sector of space, and registered like the waves of an angry sea on entropy monitors as far out as the Rim. It was a fitting expression of Kanizar's might and wrath that when he returned home to investigate news of the threat to his wife and heirs, the whole galaxy should be shaken.

Normally the shield of ships dissolved into paths leading to the vessels' home planets. On this occasion, however, the shield held steady. Only a few ships, Kanizar's flagship at their head, streaked toward Meon. Kanizar's reception was both jubilant and grave. He was full of praise for Meon's defenders, saddened by the loss of old Sashu, and apprehensive about the fate of Miram and the children. His immense victories in the campaign from which he had just returned went almost unmentioned in the face of his anger at the deeds of the Pretender.

Having a wisdom long prompted by old Sashu's hand,

Kanizar knew that loyalty was a two-edged blade. He forewent his immediate resolution to burn into space to avenge himself on the Pretender, and first made provision that the home planets should always have adequate defense. He further charged his new chancellor to dedicate a large part of his fortunes to making what restitution was possible to those who had suffered through the Pretender's coming.

Then Kanizar, the King of Kings, stole a quiet hour and walked out alone onto the Field of Perfection just as the Hub stars were beginning to show their full magnificence. By accident, he stumbled on Zim's gimbal bow, and picked it up, marveling at how straight and strong was its design, considering that the lad had constructed it himself. Nearby was Arma's little rocking cradle, containing all but one of her favorite toys. Kanizar was not a man given to showing emotion, other than superhuman anger, but when he returned to his castle he carried these playthings in his arms as though they were the bodies of the children themselves. His cheeks were unashamedly wet with tears.

That night, specially selected units of Kanizar's fleets detached themselves from the false moon in the sky and made rendezvous with Kanizar's flagship as it rose in a cold, controlled passion from Meon. When the rendezvous was complete, the avenging taskforce jumped into hyperspace with such near simultaneity that the shock to the continuum could not fail to be read by the Pretender's craft no matter in what section of the universe it lay. Kanizar said prayers to the gods of strength and terrible retribution and to a deity less known to the mighty, which the Terrans might have called hope. And these gods were invoked by every ship in the force as it burned toward the region of Ortel.

EIGHTEEN

Their trials on Avida had changed them all considerably, but none as radically as Miram. Arma was growing out of her childhood almost visibly, and showing an astonishing capability in seconding her mother at the women's chores; Zim was becoming all too suddenly a man, with the able savagery of his forefathers, and all of Kanizar's intelligence; Bogaert was finding new resources within himself unconnected with his military training—but Miram was transformed almost beyond recognition.

Her honey-gray hair, now close-cropped by the sap, showed more of her brow and revealed a face with an astonishing strength of character. Furthermore, despite the unusual diet, the harsh, active life had given her a considerable appetite. Her willowy slimness was giving way to an attractive roundness. Kanizar was going to have difficulty recognizing this tough, rounded, and increasingly practical savage as the slight doll who had graced his side through the courts of kings and emperors.

There was another change in Miram, also. Although the daily hardships and danger were of constant concern, she had learned to laugh aloud. Prompted by Bogaert's tendency to make light of the seemingly impossible, she had developed a sense of humor in adversity. Zim often looked up wonderingly when he heard his mother's laughter ring out across the clearing. He once remarked to Bogaert that, despite the circumstances, he had never remembered Miram being happier. Bogaert made no reply. He was only too conscious of her increasing attractions and of the strong bonds which were forming between them.

Although it was never discussed, they were all tacitly

agreed that there was no point in patterning their lives as though rescue would be either soon or certain. Though hopes of relief were never far from their thoughts, there was the knowledge that they had been manipulated into the situation, and that the manipulators themselves might forestall any attempt at early rescue. That a human intruder prowled around their camp was a further indication of no good will from those who had arranged the game. Bogaert therefore constructed his defenses and installations as though they had to last for years.

He spent the early hours of darkness continuing his work on the power plant, and managed to improve it to such a degree that many of the cabin instruments began to operate, if only dimly. Of particular interest was a *ransad* ground-scanning device intended to give warning of personnel near a launch pad near takeoff. The Colonel found its range amply covered the area to the fringes of the forest, and trained the others to listen for the tonal qualities which might indicate the return of the intruder or the presence of a large beast in the vicinity.

It was while examining the control cells to discover which he could use and which he could dismantle for parts that Bogaert found a considerable quantity of mercury in one of the *ransad* units. He had originally been after the transparent dome to make a supplement to his sun-powered stills, and the finding of the liquid metal was an unexpected bonus.

By altering his chlorine cell to use mercury as the negative electrode, he was able to separate the sodium from the salt water as a mercury amalgam. This reacted with pure water to form a solution of caustic soda. With the alkali and some fat recovered from spit-roasted animals, he was able to prepare a kind of soap. The product was a slimy mess, with a rancid, animal smell and a tendency to burn the skin, but, using liberal quantities of water, they were able to wash themselves properly for the first time since their arrival.

One of the main chores each day was the fetching of water from the swamp. Despite the clearance which had taken place, it was still the most dangerous part of their routine. The electric fence had to be turned off, and they had to make a passage through tracks still occasionally the haunt of savage and fast-moving animals. Now that their use of water was increasing, Bogaert and Zim were being exposed to this danger for longer periods each day. To add to the problem, a variety of fleshy herb was repopulating the cleared ground, providing cover for a number of small but dangerous animals. Attempts to burn the herb proved futile because of its high moisture content, nor was the amount of wire available sufficient to extend their protected area as far as the swamp.

Bogaert decided to dig a channel to conduct the water to a point inside the fence. The soil was a rich loam and easily disturbed, but because of the extended time involved working knee-deep in newly grown herbage, the project could not be considered unless the undergrowth was first cleared. He searched in vain through the stores in the pod, hoping to find an effective defoliant, but there was no sign that any such thing had ever been included. He next tried treating the ground with caustic soda solution, but the success was only partial. To do the job properly would have required more caustic than he was capable of producing. He therefore turned his attention to the possibility of making sodium chlorate weedkiller in his assembly of pots, wires, and pieces of metal.

Viewing the range of things that the Colonel had already produced from the crude electrolysis apparatus with a feedstock of salt water, Zim had gained the impression that it could be made to produce anything in creation. Bogaert had to admit that he had never before considered the true potential of so limited a system. Now that he could produce caustic soda, he could use the alkali in the electrolysis of water to produce both oxygen and hydrogen. These gases combined in the proportion produced by electrolysis formed an explosive mixture of creditable blasting power.

He cautiously demonstrated this fact to Zim by filling a bladder made of tied entrails and igniting the mixture with an improvised electrical fuse. The explosion stung their ears and echoed for many seconds between the distant mountains. Both were immediately impressed with its potential as a defensive weapon, and they made several more explosive balloons to test the idea. These they fixed at strategic places near the perimeter, able to fire them electrically should the need arise.

Bogaert then continued his experiments to produce sodium chlorate. By bubbling chlorine through boiling caustic, he obtained a mixture which should have contained salt and the weedkiller mixed. The effect of this on the Avidan weeds was remarkable. So promptly did they die that Miram laughingly told him that it was only a matter of time before he killed off all the vegetation on the planet. Bogaert did not laugh. He had seen what technology had done to his native Terra.

When they started to dig the swamp end of the water channel, Bogaert and Zim noticed two remarkable things. The first was an actual sight of the one they took to be the intruder, squatting on the bank of an island across the swamp. Zim raised the question of how the dark figure had gained the island, because the thick banks of slime which broke the surface of the water would have been a serious impediment to any form of boat.

The second discovery followed Bogaert's curse when his spade, biting deeply into the loam, struck something hard like a plateau of buried rock. He explored with the spade, trying to find its depth and extent. The cut took him so near to the edge of the swamp that a bank of slime gave way and flooded the hole with black and sedimented water. The instant before the water swept in, he saw something which stayed his hand in surprise: the first wash of water revealed not a stone, but a section of an elaborate mosaic pavement of undoubtedly human construction.

Immediately the scene was lost as the black water swamped the hole. He began at first to wonder if it had been a trick of his imagination. Moving back a couple of meters, he began to shovel the loam from over a broad area. Soon he was rewarded by a section of ornate paving running in a direction aslant to his intended channel and apparently continuing outward across the swamp, only shallowly covered by the waters. The line of the pavement continued to a point directly below where the enigmatic figure sat watching them. As soon as it was obvious that they had made the connection, the dark figure rose, raised one arm in a salute, and walked away among the island trees.

Zim explored the edges of the swamp and confirmed the presence of the pavement leading like a barely submerged causeway out toward the island. Meanwhile, Bogaert had scraped a section of the mosaic clean, and was examining the alien intricacy and artistry of its design. On Terra or any advanced star world, this would have been an important archeological find. On Avida, however, it represented a route by which a potentially dangerous intruder could invade their territory with impunity. Nor did Bogaert fail to make a significant connection as the sound of Miram's laughter drifted easily between the blackened trees. It was now doubly important that the Kanizars were never left without protection.

Having dug the first part of the channel, Zim and Bogaert sealed the mainland end of the causeway with a huge pile of woody thornbush, which they dragged into position with ropes and hooks because of the spitefulness of the thorns. In gathering this material, they surprised a huge feline creature which had been sleeping on the edge of the forest. A single shot from the ion gun mercifully halted a charge which they could not possibly have withstood, and reminded them of the continuing dangers of being too long outside the protection of the wire. They inspected the dead beast to see if it could possibly be used as food. Something odd about its warty skin and curious, random tufts of hair caused Bogaert to take a dislike to the carcass. He could not specifically say that the creature was diseased, but he decided that the meat would not be worth the risk.

The Colonel's judgment was proved correct when, three days later, the carcass still showed no sign of having decomposed. What factor was responsible for its continued preservation, he did not discover, but several creatures that took a meal from the carcass had died soon after they had filled their stomachs. So slight were the divisions between life and death on Avida.

NINETEEN

Aware of the fires but not of their purpose, Bethschant had that night crept into Bogey's camp, thinking to seize the woman while the Colonel and the boy were occupied at the far end of the clearing. He could have saved himself a lot of pain and trouble had he bothered first to wonder why the ring of fire had been established. By investigating more closely, he would have found that the woman he sought was also in the fire ring, but he had considered no circumstance unlikely enough to bring a woman out into the Avidan night when she had a safe shelter in which to sleep.

He had spent many hours watching the group from the shelter of the forest edge, greatly intrigued by the curious things with which Colonel Bogey occupied his time. Unexpectedly, the occupants of the barge appeared not only to be surviving but to be in positive ascendency over their Avidan environment. It was obvious that with the crucial advantage offered by the barge they had both the means and the will to remain on Avida for as long as circumstance required. He was impressed by the way the Colonel had attacked the forest rather than suffering its dangers and hardships. Bethschant reflected ruefully that, had the members of his own tribe been as positive in their approach, they might still be kings on their own planet.

Bethschant knew he could have killed Colonel Bogey several times had he chosen, and the Colonel would never have known the mode or reason of his death. Having no care about time, the native had stayed his hand, preferring to make a sport of the affair to provide some interest in the boredom of his otherwise complete isolation. He planned to steal the woman, and when the Colonel came out to the rescue, Bethschant would kill him face to face, warrior against warrior, with the woman to witness his superiority.

With this in mind, Bethschant had approached the pod from the direction opposite that of the ring of fire. He was slightly amused to find the door hatch secured from the outside with rope, a fact he took to indicate that the Colonel was having trouble containing the woman. The portent was promising: a creature of such high spirits would undoubtedly be sport to catch and tame.

Pausing outside the door, Bethschant applied his ear to the crack and heard reassuring movements within. He reasoned that the female child would be asleep, and that the woman was probably engaged in some housekeeping chore. With his long-knife Bethschant silently cut the rope, swung the panel, and leaped into the dark interior. Then, even in a darkness lit only by the dim reflection from the flames, he knew he had made the greatest mistake of his life. The dry-shelled rustle of stricken snappers was a terrifying revelation of the nature of the trap into which he had walked. His horrified comprehension was completed by a stinging in his eyes and a burning sensation in his throat.

He found it almost impossible to breathe, and, with his feet stumbling on piles of still writhing, contorted snapper bodies, Bethschant counted himself fortunate to have fallen backward out the door hatch. A clatter from the creatures in the pod warned him of pursuit, and he swung the heavy hatch behind him but fell over a pile of wire and pottery which had been heaped close by. From the pain in his throat and chest, he reasoned he had been dealt a grave injury. His eyes, swimming, refused to accept anything but the blurred image of the flames. He heard a shout from beyond the fires, and considered it probable that the Terran knew his trap had been sprung. In no condition for fighting or even for defense, Bethschant half crawled, half staggered away into the darkness, losing all his weapons in the process, intent only on finding a place where he could rest and if necessary die peacefully from the injuries to his lungs.

He found no sleep in the forest crevice into which he finally stumbled. An alarming weakness possessed his limbs, and he repeatedly coughed up quantities of frothy fluid. His head ached in a manner he had never before experienced, and he was convinced that death was slowly coming upon him. He twisted all night to deter the fibers and things which rose out of the ground to attack his body, while he prayed with every hard-won breath for the gods to save his lungs. Toward morning, the pain had slightly eased, although he still coughed considerably. He moved off slowly into the deep forest, where the air seemed cooler and moister and less painful to inhale. As the day passed, he found a gradual return to normal, though he still had to avoid undue exertion. It was a further week before he could comfortably run again.

Throughout the period of his recovery, he took great care to avoid any contact with the inhabitants of the ship. He was of two minds as to whether he had walked into a deliberate trap set for him or not. Either possibility seemed to confirm the things he had heard about the terrible Terrans. If this injury had been accidental, he hated to contemplate what Colonel Bogey could do to his enemies by design.

The loss of his cough and the capacity to breathe easily again brought the renewal of his confidence. By now the demon Colonel had succeeded in setting fire to a considerable strip of forest, and there was no cover to be had between the blackened trees until the foliage grew again. This same fact, however, worked partly to Bethschant's advantage, because it left Bogey's clearing in view from the island, and Bethschant found he could sit comfortably in the trees and watch all that went on around the pod without much fear of discovery.

He now viewed more cautiously what had at first seemed a naive act: that of putting two metal strings as a fence around the clearing. His previous experience told him Colonel Bogey was unlikely to have done such a thing without good reason. The scheme became clearer when he noted that any animal which touched the fence was usually killed by the contact. He made a note that small running-horns, which leaped between the strings, could cross the clearing with impunity. Bethschant practiced the movement over a log and beneath the fronds of an overhanging tree, until he knew he could make a similar passage without any slackening of speed.

The point prompted him to observe everything the Colonel did as closely as possible. Bogaert and the boy were hiding things in the ground and leading strings away toward the pod. Bethschant guessed these were Terran traps, and mentally marked their positions. The next time he came to take the woman, he wanted no possible chance of having to retreat in defeat.

The woman herself was the real prize. He did not know whether it was his own desire which made her seem more attractive whenever she came into view, or she was actually changing into something more akin to what Bethschant would have liked to have believed was the ideal Avidan woman. She laughed frequently, and her laughter floating across the swamp made him squirm with longing. When he had taken her and made her used to his native Avidan ways, he hoped she would still be able to laugh. His own former Avidan mate had been more nearly an animal: sullen, morose, and concerned only with the necessities of survival and what minimal comfort she could obtain. Miram (for such he had heard the others call her) was different, and her presence seemed to light the forest edge more brightly than one of Bogaert's fires.

When he thought nobody was about, Bethschant made occasional sallies toward the wire to test the defenses and have a closer look at Bogey's creations. Lately, the demon Colonel always seemed to detect his coming and open the door hatch and scan the area. Sometimes the boy would come also, with what was recognizably an ion gun. It mystified Bethschant as to why, when they had so devastating a weapon available, they did not use it more often. He concluded that the Colonel's confidence rendered the device of marginal value. Nevertheless, the native took good care to remain unseen whenever within range of ion fire.

Life had been difficult without the long-knife. It was to regain this that Bethschant planned his attack earlier than he might otherwise have done. An almost complete knowledge of Bogey's defensive system gave him confidence that the Colonel could still be taken by surprise. Bethschant reasoned that if he attacked in fading light, there would be little chance of his being visually observed even if the Colonel did have some mysterious knowledge of his approach. With a rising bravado, Bethschant no longer bothered to conceal himself when he was beyond the range of the ion gun. For this reason, he was still sitting on the island bank, interestedly watching Bogey's latest mystery, when the Colonel and the boy discovered the end of the causeway and its connection with the island.

The incident caused a point of decision for Bethschant. If the causeway gave him easy passage to the island, it would also permit Colonel Bogey and his strange weapons to make the crossing. To forestall the prospect of being hunted across the island like an animal, Bethschant decided he would attack that very evening, before the Terran was able to take advantage of the new knowledge. That the Colonel had appreciated the significance of the causeway was indicated by the fact that he had bothered to seal the mainland end with spiteful rawthorn. Bethschant, however, had his own way around the obstacle, and this could only add to the element of surprise.

The native spent the rest of the afternoon preparing his weapons. He had changed his mind about drawing the Colonel into a fight, because the Terran's policy of dealing with unwanted things appeared to be extermination rather than combat. The Colonel would have to be killed first; then the boy with the gun. Bethschant had decided to keep the female child as well as the woman, and to take over the pod in Bogey's place. So pleased was he with this idea that he could scarcely suppress his eagerness to start bringing it about. He retipped all his spears and flights with the swiftest poison he could find, and went to great lengths to arrange the decoy which would draw the Colonel and the boy out into the open.

Once the two men had cleared the shelter of the pod, with their attention focused elsewhere, Bethschant knew, from the place where he intended to conceal himself he could drop them both, swiftly and silently. Inside the pod, the woman would never know she had changed hands until her new master arrived for the feast. The best part of the fighting would take place inside the pod: taming the woman and forcing her to accept that his whim was law. If things worked out as he hoped, Bethschant thought, he might even stay on Avida and found a new dynasty when the game was ended, instead of returning to Xzan and his perpetual problems with the star worlds.

Finally, everything was prepared. Bethschant moved silently across the causeway, bearing the many things he considered he needed for the success of his venture. Reaching the mainland, he traveled a considerable way along the swamp edge before turning inland and taking a curved route that actually placed the pod between himself and the swamp. With some dexterity, he set up the woven decoy which in the closing darkness could easily be mistaken for himself. Then he crept to the place he had chosen and arranged his weapons, ready for instant use.

He was about to toss a log onto the fence, which he was certain would fetch the Colonel and the boy out to investigate, when he experienced a peculiar shimmer of his vision—a sensation with which he had become familiar during his service on the star worlds. It was a distortion of the continuum caused by one or more ships breaking out of hyperspace somewhere in the vicinity of the planet. This in itself would not have worried Bethschant overmuch, yet he paused to consider its significance. It could be Xzan come to check on the progress of the game; it could be Oontara, who already seemed to have equipped his champion with far more than was originally agreed on—or it could be that the Colonel had somehow called for rescue or reinforce-

ment from Terra. Whatever the nature of the space
visit, it was bound to have some effect on Bethschant's
present plans. The native considered it prudent to find
out what changes this new factor would introduce before he engaged in the risks of killing Bogey and captur-
ing the pod.

TWENTY

Like a trio of avenging demons, the three fastest
ships of the Pretender's fleet dropped out of hyperspace. Each carved a separate trajectory into orbit
around Avida, losing no time in starting to scan the surface for any possible clues as to the whereabouts of the
missing Kanizars.

Camin Sher was in the instrument room of the lead
ship, cursing the reluctance of his space technicians to
give hope of locating three or four individuals on an
entire planet. Nor, from the nature of the terrain which
the optical instruments depicted, was it obvious that
better results would be yielded by a ground search unless the approximate area could first be determined.
The whole proposition appeared hopeless—a fact
which Sher had not appreciated until his arrival.

Despite the unassailable logic of this argument, they
were wrong. At a point close to the terminator, the
communications technicians found evidence of a ground
scanner at work. The transmissions were diffuse, because the radiation was not directed skyward but reflected from objects on the ground. Nevertheless, on an
otherwise uninhabited planet, any evidence of wave
transmission was evidence of human life. After securing
a tentative fix for the position, Camin Sher ordered a
landing party to go down.

The Pretender gave charge of the landing party to
Pera Hai, his second in command. His reasons for doing

so were twofold. There had recently been signs that Hai himself was beginning to doubt the Pretender's prospects of succeeding Kanizar. Sher considered it good politics to give Hai the task of attending to the executions. There was also the slight chance that, if the Terran lived up to his reputation, Hai might be killed. Either ending was acceptable to the Pretender. Hai would either be convinced of Sher's cause by witnessing the removal of Kanizar's heirs, or else the death of Hai would relieve Sher of a dangerous nucleus of apostasy in his ranks.

Because there were no ferry ships and no landing pads available, they were forced to make planetfall using lifecraft. Hai chose to take only twelve hand-picked men in full battle order, to create a tight commando force which he could oversee as a body. Something in Sher's own reticence to lead the attack twisted a cautious knot in Hai's stomach, and made him take more than ordinary care with his preparations. Avida had an evil reputation, but he was not sure whether Camin Sher, the wildlife, or the mysterious Colonel Bogey was the factor most to be feared.

From his position back on the forest's edge, Bethschant heard the lifecraft fall. Once into the atmosphere, it had applied ionization braking, and there was little to mark its actual descent other than the sharp crackle of static as it passed overhead. It made planetfall about three kilometers away, in the trees. There was a reasonable chance that the occupants of the pod had missed the craft's coming, unless they had had reason to anticipate its fall. From the lack of activity around the pod, Bethschant guessed that they had slept.

Interested in the purpose of the visit, Bethschant silently made his way toward the lifecraft, his curiosity causing him to take chances in passing through black forest recesses which were better avoided until daylight. As was usual at night, the forest was alive with all manner of creatures, many of which lived in deep burrows during the day. Many of the major predators were nocturnal, and the routines of hunting and being hunted filled the forest spaces with unimaginable animal sounds. Through this natural bedlam, Bethschant's keen ears began to detect sounds of men and equipment being readied for movement. He judged there to be about a dozen men with full space armor and equipment packs. He smiled wryly as he considered how inappropriate these items were for service on Avida.

Soon he came across the group, making heavy work of forging a path through the forest instead of taking advantage of natural weakness in the brush. He found that he could move around them in the darkness quite easily, and take advantage of the restrictions to their senses imposed by their armor to approach quite closely without fear of detection. One of the men was using a communicator pack, presumably in contact with the ship in orbit. He periodically gave the leader course instructions, and it was obvious from their general direction that those in the ship had a fair idea of the location of the pod.

The first calamity for the party came when, in hacking a path under a large tree, one of the shipmen put a long-knife through a bite-wing nest. Bethschant heard the characteristic scream of angry wings and retired to a discreet distance. The men from the lifecraft were not so lucky. At least three of the shipmen must have opened the face-bulbs of their helmets in order to cope with the high humidity. This presented the bite-wings with targets upon which to avenge the injury to the nest. The men's screams did not last long. Bethschant could have told them it would be only a matter of half an hour before the three suits of armor would contain nothing but bones.

Had the bite-wings attacked Bethschant, he would have crashed through the brush, twisting and rolling as he went, to make the ferns and twigs strike the creatures from his body. Distance also was of paramount importance, because even starving bite-wings never traveled far from the swarm. A fast-running man could normally escape with only a few bites. Colonel Bogey had had the foresight to burn a large area of forest clear of nesting wildlife, and thus had not encountered the problem. The soldiers, however, had damaged a nest and then remained in the vicinity. Three whipcrack bursts of ion fire told how their leader had finally decided to solve the problem.

When the party was clear of the bite-wing nest, Bethschant crept closer and counted the survivors—now only ten, including the leader. He climbed a low branch of a tree along their intended route and tried to hear their conversation as they passed. He heard the name "Miram" mentioned several times, and formed the impression that this must be a rescue party come to take the woman back to the stars. With his own plans for the woman well advanced, Bethschant was not prepared to consider any chance of having her prematurely taken from the scene. He decided to assist Avida in the work of destruction which the wildlife had already started.

One native against ten armed and armoured shipmen was not the daunting prospect it appeared. Bethschant knew the ways of the forest, had the advantage of mobility even in darkness, and the benefit of surprise. Furthermore, from his service with Xzan, he well knew the shipmen's equipment and armor and the nature of their defenses. His prime target was the man with the communicator. No one could have seen or heard the upthrusting spear which penetrated the fellow's body armor at the vulnerable waist joint, but the communications man staggered into the brush and died. When his colleagues discovered where the body had fallen, the poisoned shaft had been removed and the communicator was nowhere to be found. Bethschant counted on his fingers. Only nine shipmen remained.

There followed an anguished conference, with some shipmen urging a return and their leader pointing out that without the communicator to give them guidance they would be unlikely to find their way back to the lifecraft again before daylight. He then ordered the mission to continue, and the complaining party once again went ahead.

When Bogaert had managed to set fire to the forest, the flames had traveled inland from the swamp edge for a great distance before reaching a region of mud banks and quagmires which acted as a firebreak. It was on the far side of this same obstacle that the shipmen now emerged. In the darkness, the sluggish rivulets were not distinguishable from open patches of terrain, and two of the shipmen were lost by drowning in the slow mud drains before the leader called a halt and decided to remain in the same spot until daybreak. Without the communicator, he was unable to transmit this decision to the ship, and in their attempts to find a way around the treacherous mires they had effectively lost their bearings.

With the party now reduced to seven, afraid to open their armor for any reason, it was a demoralized group that waited for the dawn. Bethschant climbed into a tree above them and tried to encourage a fast-creeper to disentangle from the branches and drop upon them, but the sentient vegetable refused to consider the armor-clad shipmen edible. This failure did not worry the native overmuch. He had a shrewd idea that confinement in the armor was becoming insufferable, and he was gaining the feeling that, because of their tolerance to their losses, this was more likely to be a raiding than a rescue party. This latter point implied that Colonel Bogey's defenses would probably add to the death toll, leaving Bethschant to deal with only a few survivors to insure that no harm came to the woman.

This suited Bethschant better than his earlier plan. Because of the appalling lack of fieldcraft exhibited by the shipmen, he was confident of his ability to kill them at any moment he chose. If the shipmen themselves could deal with the dreadful Colonel, then his main problem was solved.

Dawn broke, and the uncertain light grew stronger. The unhappy warriors rose, shook stiff limbs, and continued to plot a path around the mud holes which would lead them into the newly grown herbage of the burned forest strip. Once among the blackened trees, they appreciated the reduction in wildlife and became brave enough to open their face-bulbs and even remove their helmets altogether. Keeping low in the new vegetation,

Bethschant shadowed them silently with a wry anticipation of what was to follow.

At the sight of the pod standing in the clearing, the party again became a military team. The leader gave detailed instructions as to the method of attack and the angle of approach. Two were sent ahead to gain positions on the swamp side of the clearing, while the remainder separated and took places along the landward side. At a signal, they began a simultaneous advance. Bethschant made no attempt to follow, but climbed the blackened stump of a tree to gain a better view. The first man to touch the fence died as the animals had done, and another on the far side of the clearing, unable to see the fate of his comrade, likewise met his end.

Thereafter, the fence was destroyed in several places by ion fire, and the advance continued, with the leader calling on the Colonel to surrender the Kanizars. A device which Bethschant had not known about exploded close to one of them, and the five survivors now became four. Two turned and ran, and Bethschant's arrows straight into the vulnerable waist-joint of their suits dropped them in mid-stride. Another reached the door of the pod, intending to wrench it open. He met a close-range burst of ion fire directed expertly through the opening gap, and dropped like a falling log. Only the leader now remained. He turned and ran toward the nearest clump of trees outside the clearing.

This was an unwise move, as Bethschant could have told him. Colonel Bogey had something hidden in those trees which the native had never understood, but which certainly formed some sort of trap. The sound of an explosion low in the trees signaled that the demon Colonel had recognized the advantage. The running man faltered, threw his hands protectively over the open bulb of his helmet, then began to stagger blindly, all further thoughts of flight forgotten.

Although Bethschant could not see what manner of injury had struck the leader, it was certain that the man was in very great pain. Something invisible had stopped the fully armed space warrior and turned him into a blind, defeated creature. When the Colonel and the boy appeared at the door hatch, Bethschant retreated into the forest. The action had not gone at all the way he had hoped, and his respect for the terrible Terran was increasing by the hour.

TWENTY-ONE

From Bogaert's point of view, several members of the attacking force were still not accounted for. Emerging cautiously from the door hatch, he crouched low and ran to where one of the men had been blasted by an oxy-hydrogen mine which had been buried below the approach to the pod. The explosive power of the buried gas bomb should not have been sufficient to kill a man in armor, but the blast had lifted the fellow bodily, and landed him with a broken neck. An ion carbine was the Colonel's gratifying gain.

Still low on the ground, Bogaert surveyed the area warily, trying to estimate the extent of any further attack by counting the number of fallen. Two had been electrocuted by the wire, one blasted by the mine, one shot by Zim, and one was even now staggering from the effects of a faceful of strong caustic solution distributed by a gas mine concealed in a tree. The Colonel's estimation from the ground scanner had been seven men, with a possible eighth slightly out of range. Potentially there could be three attackers still to come.

Zim doubled out to the wire to collect the weapons of the men who had fallen there. Bogaert permitted him to make this dangerous sortie because he had discovered that the lad's field sense was even better than his own. What Bogaert had not anticipated was that Zim would suddenly stand and begin to beckon with his arms. Bogaert shouted to him to keep low, and ran over to see what had so excited the boy's attention. When he arrived he found two further members of the attack party dead on the ground, with native arrow shafts sticking out precisely from the waist joints of their armor. For a certainty, the eighth man who had shown on the scanner had been their native antagonist, who, for reasons of his own, appeared to have chosen to attack the newcomers rather than assist them.

This came as a surprise to Bogaert, who had assumed the attacking party were Xzan's own men. On closer inspection he decided their insignia was that of Camin Sher, the Pretender. Whereas he had supposed the threat to be against his own life, it was now obvious that the Kanizars were the target. Furthermore, if a small task force had landed, it was certain a larger force was still in orbit.

He turned back to the unfortunate who had run into the caustic dispersion liberated by the gas mine in the tree, and sent Zim scurrying for water. The facial burns were going to be serious, because the fellow had opened the bulb of his helmet as he ran. Certainly nothing could now save his sight. If Bogaert felt any pity, it was quelled by the thought that the man was a member of an armed murder party sent to kill a woman and two children.

Miram herself brought the water and carefully washed and cleansed the burns. Bogaert and Zim helped the shipman out of his armor—but it was little Arma, full of solicitude for his plight, who took the blind warrior's hand and led him back toward the pod. When he was seated, she brought him food and a drink of water, and her own bean-filled cushion, which he declined.

Although blind and in extreme pain, the shipman looked up as Bogaert came in, recognizing a military step.

"Are you in league with the gods, Colonel Bogey?" he asked with difficulty. "Else why does everything on this cursed planet rush to your aid?"

"You'd not think it did if you were in our position," said Bogaert, settling himself on a sack next to the stricken man.

"Believe me, it's true. We were thirteen when we left

the lifecraft. The wildlife, the landscape, and the natives halved our number before we even reached here."

"You're Pera Hai, Sher's lieutenant, aren't you?"

"Do you read minds, also?"

"No. I've been reading the document foil in your armor. How many men has the Pretender in orbit?"

"By this time, better than twenty thousand."

"Yet he sent only thirteen?"

"Sher sensed trouble. That's why he didn't come himself. We were goats thrust in to test the extent of danger. We lost our communicator early, so we've not reported back, thus confirming Sher's fears. His next move'll be a space strike."

"I wonder he didn't do that first." Bogaert reverted to the role of tactician.

"It complicates the issue," said Hai. "To succeed, he needs proof of his claims of assassination. It's difficult to find convincing proof in a bomb crater. Even when he does make a strike, he'll have to do it delicately, else he'll have nothing to show the doubting kings he wishes to influence."

"You're an easy man to talk to, Hai. You've told me a lot without close questioning. Why?"

"Because the Pretender's cause is lost, and he knows I'm convinced of it. Thus he plotted me out of his way. I wasn't intended to survive this exercise."

"Would you have been convinced of the Pretender if this assassination had succeeded?"

The blind warrior screwed up his face with the pain of his burns. "There's more to being King of Kings than successful murder of women and children. It's a question of stature."

"Stature?"

"Great star rulers are born, not self-elected. True dominance gathers in the bloodline through centuries of successful combat. The young Kanizar shot my warrior through a door crack no wider than the ion beam. The shot was impressive, but not as impressive as the battle light on the lad's face as the door opened wider. I knew then with dreadful certainty that the Pretender couldn't win."

He turned away to face outward through the hatch and continued speaking reflectively.

"I ran into your infernal device, Colonel. And a woman with kind hands treated my wounds like one the gods have sent. She also was a Kanizar. And a child whom I should have killed took my arm and scolded me like a toy. She rested me out of the sun and brought me meat. This none but a Kanizar could have done. Contrast it with the shallow wantonness of Camin Sher, and there's no doubting who'll prevail. That's why I'm honored to die at the hands of a Kanizar."

"There's no question of your dying at Zim's hands," said Bogaert. "Only from your wounds, for which we don't have medical supplies."

"I'll die all too surely when the Pretender comes. You've got to get away from here, Colonel. Sher will soften the whole area with bombs and then send a major task force to sift for evidence of the Kanizars' deaths."

"There's no way we can survive in the forest without the things available here."

"And it's certain death at Sher's hands if you remain. What about the barge—can't it still fly?"

"The power plant shut itself down during the crash. I've been able to open it up a bit, but there's nothing like full power available."

"If you have enough power to render the wire lethal, you should have sufficient for an atmospheric flight. A hop of a hundred kilometers should make it difficult for Sher to find you. He'd not have found you yet had you not been using the ground scanner. A ship's a remarkably small thing on the ground when you're looking for it from orbit."

"You're making sense, Hai. Except I've no idea how to fly the thing. I fetched her down by inactivating the ghost and switching to a preset landing mode. I don't know enough of the *ransad* to pilot the thing even as an atmospheric craft."

"But I do, Colonel. Take me with you. I'll be the brains, you the eyes. Between us, we could make it."

"Possibly. But why should you want to help us?"

"I'm a stricken man, and blind. I've no further use for the Pretender, nor he for me. If I can't die at the hands of a Kanizar, at least let me not suffer extermination by Camin Sher."

"You change sides with remarkable alacrity."

"There's no time to argue the case," said Hai tiredly. "You can take a chance and trust me, or you can wait for the murderer to come."

"We don't have much choice."

"I've a further suggestion, Colonel. Abandon the pod. With luck, Sher's bombs will blast it apart. It'll then take some while sifting the wreckage before he knows for certain you've escaped. If they discover no ship wreckage, they'll start a wider search immediately."

"The chances of our surviving without the pod are vanishingly small."

"Not as small as if you take it. A blance of risks. Every hour you buy could be crucial. I doubt Kanizar's far behind the Pretender."

"Very well! We'll give it a try. If we ever do get out of this alive, I'll see you guaranteed safe harbor."

Hai made some attempt at reply, then bit his words back and kept the comment to himself. Bogaert went to explain the situation to the others. The prospect of piloting the craft on an atmospheric trip, guided by a blind former enemy, did not give him much ease. The idea of having to continue living on Avida without the protection and facilities of the pod made him view the whole prospect with distinct apprehension. Nevertheless, Hai was unarguably right, and Bogaert therefore presented the case to Miram with a confidence he did not feel.

TWENTY-TWO

Hai predicted that the best time for an undetected takeoff would be at sunset, when cooling of the atmosphere would introduce distortions in many of the observations being made from the orbiting ships. In any case, it was nearing sunset before the two men, sitting in the powerbarge cabin, managed to evolve a system of communication which made makeshift use of Bogaert's eyes and hands and Hai's eyeless knowledge. Having defined which of the instrument cells were necessary for atmospheric-flight information, Bogaert had to keep up a continuous commentary on their indicated state, while reacting immediately and precisely to Hai's directions. Their rehearsals showed grave deficiencies in the system, but there was no time for improvement.

Miram and the children had been sorting their possessions to decide which were the absolute necessities they should attempt to take. Now, clutching a nucleus of food, water, tools, and arms, they forced their way into the already crowded cabin. It was immediately obvious that the captured ion carbines, valuable though they might be, were a physical danger in such cramped conditions. Reluctantly Bogaert dropped all but one back down into the pod before closing and sealing the hatch. Then came the point he had been dreading. Squatting before the instrument cells, he began calling the indications and listening for Hai's directions.

He severed the connections with the pod correctly, but allowed the reaction power to build too fast. The craft left the ground with a bone-shaking punch instead of a controlled acceleration, and Arma whimpered with fright. Bogaert fought the controls but overcompensated, though at least he managed to maintain the craft on an even keel. Then, under the guiding influence of

129

Hai, who maintained a fatalistic calm, he managed to re-trim for horizontal flight, and began to look about for the most promising direction in which to fly.

Attracted by the noise, Bethschant watched the barge ascend. At first he had the notion that it might be trying to escape past the orbiting ships and make for Ortel or another star world. The barge, however, hovered uncertainly at no great height and then set off in the direction of the broken hills. The native moved out from his cover into the open and followed its progress with interested eyes.

Because the distance was extreme for so small an object, he could not be certain, but he thought he saw it fall to the ground again, and memorized a few landmarks to guide his direction when he chose to follow. Firstly, however, he wanted to have a look at the abandoned pod itself. This time he did not fear traps, because from the manner of their leaving it was obvious that the party had no intention of returning.

Bethschant had no reason to explain why the pod had been left behind. Clearly it made so excellent a shelter that it had enabled its recent occupants to survive with only a fraction of the risks and discomfort that had beset the nomad. He surveyed the progress the Colonel had made toward taming the forest in so short a time, and accepted the implied rebuke that he and his kind could have made a similar stand had they known it was possible and had they an idea how it might have been achieved. He finished his tour with the firm resolve that he, Bethschant, was going to see Avida repopulated, and this time it would be the wildlife which would have to withdraw. Perhaps the Terrans might even lend him someone terrible, like Colonel Bogey, to make the forests cringe and the animals die magically at the touch of a wire.

So strong was this resolution and so appealing its goal that the native determined to start changing his way of life immediately. The abandoned pod offered a far better camp than he could build. Much of the food he found was already prepared, but he needed fresh meat to supplement the grain and paste cakes, and therefore a hunting trip was necessary. He considered using one of the ion carbines for the hunt, but realized the noise of the weapon would preclude a second shot should the first one fail. He therefore took his bow and spears and started off into the forest to secure his supper before the darkness closed. The move was fortuitous, because scarcely was he safely between the trees when the whole area was rocked by a string of bombs which leaped down from space.

Dazed and shaken by the intensity of the blasts, Bethschant lay for a long while pressed to the ground, then circled warily until he was reasonably sure that no more were going to fall. A line of splintered trees now blocked his path, but he pressed carefully through the broken timbers until he could see the site. Where the pod had stood there was now a monstrous hole surrounded by seven smaller craters whose edges literally overlapped.

Such precision bombing from space was no magic to the native. He had seen it employed many times in the course of his service with Xzan. What did suprise him was the number of bombs employed against an individual target when one would have been sufficient. Could it be that those in the ships felt it necessary to take no possible chance that the occupants of the pod might survive? And what would their reaction be when they realized they had failed?

There was no longer anything to retain his interest in the vicinity now the pod had been destroyed. Because of the approach of night, he now had no time in which to establish a new camp, and so he set off back over the flooded causeway to his island retreat, where he still had a tree already prepared. The loss of the pod annoyed him greatly, because it was a wanton act. Colonel Bogey had abandoned it, and those in the ships above had no use for it, yet now it had been blasted apart. He sensed that the bombs had come because the landing raid had failed. The pity was that the bombers had not known or cared about his existence or the importance of the hull to his plans for the future.

The situation defined those in the ships as enemies. They had come between him and his acquisition of the woman, and also destroyed the only realistic shelter on the planet. As he settled, still hungry, on the branches of his tree, Bethschant decided he hated these people nearly as much as he respected Colonel Bogey. He had gained the strongest regard for the Colonel's almost fanatical ability to construct a semblance of order out of chaos, whereas those in the ships had shown no talent other than a penchant to destroy.

Something happened in the night which caused Bethschant to untie himself from the branches and climb down and extinguish the slow fire beneath. The circumstance which gave rise to this action was the sound of the arrival of an incredible number of lifecraft. Over a period of about an hour, the descents continued until the native could easily have believed that as many as a hundred craft had been landed within a radius of a kilometer of the site. He took a considerable delight in the thought that inevitably a high proportion of these must have come down in the swamp. From what he knew of the foibles of lifecraft, few of these were ever likely to struggle back out of the dark waters.

Fortunately, no lifecraft landed on or near the island. Bethschant was content to remain in his cover until the nearing of dawn. At first light, he climbed down from the tree and began to explore. He detected several groups of shipmen moving toward the area where the pod had been, and one group already engaged in setting up lights around the craters to reinforce the dim shades of early morning. All were armed with ion carbines, and Bethschant gave little for his chances if he remained in the area as the search pattern closed. The occasional whiporack of ion fire echoing back from the hills was an indication that some parties were already firing at animals or shadows in the dark spaces of the great forests.

It was therefore with infinite caution that he stole across the causeway, circled the blasted pod site, and began to trek away through the forest, his sharp senses alert for any sign which might indicate the presence of other groups of men. The general direction of his travel was toward the landmarks against which he had thought the powerbarge had made its descent. Wide detours were necessary, in order to avoid several landed life-craft whose occupants were not converging on the original site but apparently were making extensive searches of the forest. The implication was that those searching the site were not convinced that the former occupants of the pod had died when the area had been blasted. From the way the search was patterned around the area, Bethschant judged that they had missed the point that the powerbarge had been reactivated and flown well out of the vicinity.

Some of the lifecraft had been set down at an even greater radius, and here random local searches were being carried out, generally without much enthusiasm because of the low probability of their producing any useful results. The activity of the wildlife had enforced the wearing of full armor, and the growing heat of the sun combined with the high humidity must have made the task extremely uncomfortable. The armor made the men noisy and abusive, and thus easy to detect from a distance. Bethschant gradually abandoned concealment for speed, frequently breaking into a trot in the more open forest spaces.

He was himself having trouble with the wildlife, which seemed particularly virulent in this area. Additionally, two of the weird creatures from the northern badlands were prowling the area, and there were many examples of the wanton killing of running-horns and razor-horns which had been torn to pieces but not eaten. Bethschant looked at this meat regretfully but dared not touch it, knowing there was no escape from the poisons distributed by the terrible badlands beasts. Instead, he fed himself while on the move by picking young shoots and berries. It was a lengthy and unsatisfying meal, but gave him the advantage of continuing movement.

It was his intention to be out of the forest and on the rising footlands below the hills before the end of light. The colder climate on the exposed and rising slopes was not favored by the forest-dwelling beasts, and though the hills contained their own brands of terror, these were mainly larger creatures which an alert man could detect and hope to avoid or kill. One did not build a camp on the hills, but rather chose a good position for defense and slept with open eyes.

As he approached the edge of the forest, Bethschant discovered another disadvantage of the more open sites. So far away and still that he had not detected it at first, a solitary lifecraft had landed on a high plateau. From this point of vantage, it had a perfect view of the sparser terrain which Bethschant was now crossing. The native knew nothing of its existence until he had betrayed both his presence and his direction of travel. He presumed he was being watched through powerful optical instruments, because the figures which emerged from the distant lifecraft split into two groups, one designed to intersect his path and the other to cover a retreat.

Bethschant had no intention of retreating, nor was he likely to walk into so obvious a trap. He changed direction subtly, so that the watchers might not know that they too had been seen, and set a new route to his destination. He estimated that he could safely pass between the encircling groups of men and still gain a useful lead. The idea of having a trail of armed shipmen following him across the open hillside was one he did not relish, but he knew that once he reached the more broken ground the advantage would be with him rather than with an armored warrior. He therefore led his pursuers determinedly toward the crown-tops of the nearer hills.

TWENTY-THREE

The diversion of the powerbarge from its original rendezvous had resulted in Avida's becoming an unusual focus of galactic interest. From a base around Sol, a task force of the Federation Navy had leaped into hyperdrive on the first leg of its vast journey to the Hub in response to Commissioner Rounding's urgent summons. The Commissioner himself was already well on his way to Avida in Oontara's space bark. In front of him now, clear on the screens, six of Xzan's wicked-looking battle craft scurried through the dimensionless tunnels of hyperspace, intent on trying to salvage the star lord's stake in the survival game.

In orbit around Avida, no less than a dozen of the Pretender's ships already held station, and several hundred of the slower vessels were following in formation. Camin Sher himself was growing anxious. After his initial exultation at finding the powerbarge, he had struck a hiatus. The superlative accuracy of his space combing had apparently destroyed the pod completely, and despite the high rewards he had offered for positive proof of the deaths of Miram and her children, none of his men had yet come forth with a claim. The crew searching the site reported that the fragments of wreckage did not warrant the conclusion that the powerbarge had been destroyed along with the pod. If the powerbarge proved to be missing, the chances were very high that Colonel Bogey had used it to transfer his royal charges elsewhere.

This was a conclusion which caused the Pretender no joy. At worst, the missing group had a whole planet on which to hide themselves, and the Terran was unlikely to repeat the mistake of using the ground scanner whose signals had attracted the first attack. There was also the curious matter of what had befallen Hai and his landing party, which had ceased to communicate shortly after starting the expedition. With the threat of Kanizar's retribution growing ever closer, and yet no gain to show for the immense risks of the undertaking, Sher began to sense that, even without Hai, parts of his force were coming very close to mutiny.

The Pretender desperately needed a piece of luck to restore his credibility; he was certain that otherwise, when the time came for a showdown with Kanizar, a large portion of his fleet would desert. He was caught between opposing opinions that either the children had been destroyed in such a manner as to leave no trace, or else they had escaped. If the first was true, his cause was already lost. He therefore grasped at the second idea, and sent an increasing number of men to the surface of the planet, in the hope that some shred of evidence would be found. Such was his need for information that he promised rewards of amazing magnitude for the man or group who made a positive find.

Even with the unorthodox scheme for its control, the flight of the powerbarge might have been a success had it not been for an unforeseen event. Once he had grown used to the feel of the controls, Bogaert found the craft a remarkably simple thing to fly—a characteristic consistent with its ease of maneuverability around a spaceport. The factor which the Terran had overlooked concerned the power plant itself.

In restoring the power from the unit, he had forced the plates apart and propped them with metal wedges. What he had not known was that the force tending to bring the plates together was proportional to the energy being drawn from the unit. The metal props had been ample to resist the compulsive force of his purely electrical usage; the reactive power needed for flight, however, was a demand many orders of magnitude greater. The powerbarge had scarcely achieved a reasonable height before the props began to flatten and distort.

Hai deduced the imminence of failing power from the engine note before Bogaert had time to sing out the readings from the instrument cells. His instruction was immediate: to hold a position above the nearest apparently flat space and let the craft ride down under its slowly decreasing reactive thrust. The incident happened at a particularly difficult time, when they had left the forest and the gentler slopes and were poised over a broken and fragmented mountain range. The only flat surface in the vicinity was a small, bare rock plateau which sloped at an uncertain angle.

A further complication which Bogaert had not anticipated was the erratic turbulence of the atmosphere over the mountains, which thrust randomly against the failing powerbarge and threatened to turn it aside from its minute landing point. With the power fading fast, Bogaert risked a little of the remaining thrust in a desperate attempt to swing the craft sideways and back onto the plateau. A gust of wind helped momentarily, and with a prayer of relief he settled the craft down only a few meters from a perilous edge.

Almost at once it became apparent that the position was unstable. The angle of the slope combined with the gusting turbulence rocked and shifted the craft in a way that made it certain that only minutes would see the barge unseated and plunging down into the broken teeth of a fractured mountain cleft. There was nothing Bogaert could do but order immediate evacuation. The jagged rock faces many hundreds of meters below foreswore that neither the craft nor the occupants would survive such a fall.

Because of the crush of bodies in the cabin, rapid evacuation was difficult. Zim and Arma managed to extricate themselves and drop down through the hatch to the ground. Miram followed, pleading for speed. Bogaert turned to the blinded Hai and tried to guide him, but the shipman shook his hand away and bade him go first. As the Terran went down through the hatch, he had the distinct impression that Hai had stood up and was groping for the control panel. Divining a pattern in the move, Bogaert joined the others on the ground and made them run hastily across the rocky face away from the vicinity of the powerbarge.

He was scarcely a moment too soon. They were barely clear of the flux-reaction field when the motors were restarted and the craft lurched sickly into flight again. For a moment it hung in the air like a wounded thing, then slewed at right angles and made a long, powered crash dive over the broken rocks into some unseen depths far below.

Miram's cry of horror and apprehension was quenched by the expression on Bogaert's face.

"That's the way he wanted it, Miram. He wasn't a man who could live without sight. It was the last thing he could do to help us."

"Help us?" Her understanding failed her. "He's robbed us of the powerbarge."

"Without the pod, we couldn't have lived in it. And it's what the Pretender will be looking for. When it's found, the search will concentrate in that area rather than here. It'll give us an extra chance."

"What chance? We've no food, no shelter, and no weapons."

"At least we're alive. We'll tackle the rest of the problems as they arise."

"Don't you Terrans ever give up hope?"

"Not till we've exhausted all possible avenues. At this juncture, we've not even got around to defining the problems."

During this conversation Bogaert had been looking round the broken terrain, trying to judge what their next move ought to be. Unquestionably, they had to descend from the plateau as quickly as possible, because the high rock was completely devoid of anything which might contribute to the maintenance of life. The air was thin, and with the waning of the sun, a bitter chill was beginning to inhabit the updrafts and blustering winds which plagued its desolation. Fortunately, the height gave them a slightly longer period of evening light than would have been available in the forest.

One face of the sloping plateau gave way to a random ramp of broken rock leading down to the foot of a sheer cliff which had itself been cleaved as if by a mighty ax. It was to this point that Bogaert decided to descend before nightfall, in the hope that the walls of rock would give some protection from the wind. The descent was difficult and dangerous, but they had all become accustomed to hardship. Even little Arma struggled on with an animallike determination which must have taxed her resources to the limit. Somehow, after what seemed a whole lifetime of exertion, they gained the foot of the cliff and began to explore the entrance to the cleft which promised some respite from the mountain winds.

The last part of the climb had been carried out in the near-darkness of the night. The passage into the cleft proved darker still. Only a narrow streak of starlight above their heads provided any evidence that they were not in fact in a cave. However, the stellar illumination was entirely insufficient to light their way. Groping with his hands and feeling the ground carefully with his feet, Bogaert pressed ever more deeply into the cleft, because the atmosphere was decidedly warmer between the narrow confines of the rocky walls. The need for warmth was paramount. Arma's reserves must have been dangerously low, and Zim, in his state of near nudity, was particularly liable to suffer from exposure.

This high in the mountains they had seen no sign of wildlife, and Bogaert prayed that they would meet none in the darkness. The only weapon they now possessed was Zim's single-shot ion gun, which hardly qualified as a reliable means of defense. Though strewn with large boulders, the underlying ledge was reasonably level, as though they were walking on a natural rock fault which had been formed when the mountain split in half. All the time he was able to feel the rocky walls on both sides and a solid floor beneath, Bogaert had not worried that they might step into an unseen precipice, but when the distance between the walls grew greater, he had no such reassurance. There he decided that further progress in the darkness did not constitute a reasonable risk, and brought the party to a halt.

There was little question of sleeping. They huddled together to conserve their natural warmth, and rearranged such tattered clothing as they still possessed to drape the outermost parts of those who were most exposed. Such a concentration of animal warmth made their wretched condition at least tolerable, and enabled the group to find a minimal comfort in a situation where an individual might have suffered dangerous chill. Arma and Zim even appeared to doze a little, though Bogaert and Miram found no such respite and spent the long night quietly discussing their predicament in tones they hoped showed no sign of panic.

Their worst period came with the slow break of dawn. A change in the mountain winds caused a bitter draft to penetrate the cleft and chill them cruelly at a time when their resistance was at its lowest. It was Bogaert's opinion that movement would be better than inactivity, and he coaxed the party back to life. They formed a very sorry and pitiful-looking band as they attempted to drape the rotting rags around themselves. Any semblance of a civilized condition refused to become discernible, and it was with the appearance of a troupe of ragged savages that they reluctantly turned their feet again to the path. Fortunately, this generated a vein of ironic humor which helped to buoy their descending spirits as they set out to discover what this newest day in the survival game would bring.

As the sky became brighter, it was possible to see a streak of light in front of them, marking the far edge of the mountain. What lay beyond, whether a sheer drop or a more gentle slope, it was impossible to decide, but the prospect lured them with more hope than logic would have dictated. There were bad rock falls to be climbed, and in their weakened condition the going was extremely hard, especially for little Arma. Thus, the sun was high in the sky before they finally broke from their rocky confines and stood to gaze with a kind of wonder at this new place they had found.

TWENTY-FOUR

Between the cradling palms of mountain ranges, a green valley sloped from their present position down to where a further outcrop separated it from the plains and forests far below. It took no great measure of observation to note that, for Avida, this valley was unusual. Because of its high location and moderate climate, the patterns of bush and fern and tree were completely unlike those of the forest floor, and in the lush, abundant grasses razor-horns grazed openly, as if unused to attack.

Nor was this the only point of note. Feeding the stream, a swift mountain cataract poured crystal waters from some mountain height into a rocky pool, from which it escaped by half a dozen channels before continuing in a swift race down to the forests and the swamplands far below. Cautiously noting the coldness of the water, Bogaert inspected the pool closely, anticipating what he would find. The water was undefiled by fleshworms and the myriad horrors of the lower swamps. Imitating the razor-horns at the stream below him, he first took a sip of the water, and then a deeper drink, then encouraged the others to do the same. After the tepid distilled water on which they had existed for so long, the draft of recently melted snow as it tumbled from the heights was a bittersweet delight.

Here in the high pass, with the sun warming their bodies despite the chill of the clear, thin air, their spirits soon revived, and the shadows of death fell away with this new promise of continued life. Their next problem was food, which, in the absence of any means of raising fire, would be necessarily limited to such fruits and berries as they already know to be safe to eat. The abundance of the horned creatures tempted them to think of meat, but although the animals seemed docile, the sharp edges of their horns promised risk of severe injury to anyone making an attack without sufficient preparation. Zim wished to shoot one. Bogaert restrained him, because they had no way yet to cook a carcass. In any case he wished to avoid any unnecessary ion fire, which might attract unwanted attention. Therefore, they ate a cold, vegetarian meal as they continued their exploration.

Reviewing his survival priorities, Bogaert decided that this high valley offered considerably easier living prospects than a return to the forests, and, because the climate was colder, their paramount need was for a shelter in which to spend the nights. They therefore moved systematically along one of the rocky walls of the valley where many overhangs and projections promised at least a roof and one wall ready-made. They were luckier than they had anticipated, coming upon an overhang which covered an almost hemispherical rock chamber open at one side only, which had the promise of even deeper cavities beyond. Nothing about the fine silt on the floor gave any reason to suppose that the place was inhabited or even visited by predators, and the entrance looked easy to defend. They therefore decided to use this as their base.

Looking carefully at their new-found habitat, Bogaert was struck by the smooth regularity of the walls. It was possible, he thought, that this was one of a chain of immense lava bubbles which, on approaching the surface of the mountain, had had an entrance cut by rain and wind erosion. He first thought that the inner chambers might be an occasional watercourse, active at some subterranean flood level, but there was no suggestion of this in the patterning of the sand or rock, and he had more pressing problems than geological speculation with which to contend.

Their vegetable meal had been time-consuming and unsatisfying. Therefore, fire and meat were the next two items on the list. With the facilities offered by the pod and the powerbarge, fire had not before been a major problem. However, in their new-found state of reduction to primitive resources, what had previously seemed simple had now become peculiarly difficult. Bogaert's first thought was to try to make fire using a bow to turn a shaft in a tinder block. He found tinder and wood for the bow without difficulty, but nothing which would serve as a string for the bow.

After blistering his fingers in a series of futile attempts to generate sufficient heat by turning the stick between the palms of his hands, he paused to take off his wrist chronometer. The sight of the curved glass covering the digital display gave him a new idea. He pried the glass from the front of the case, laid it on the ground, and dripped water into it, being careful to raise a slight meniscus. In this way, he made a small but adequate burning glass, which he held carefully over his dry tinder. He had a reasonable fire going within ten minutes.

He experimented for a while with various types of brushwood, trying to discover which burned with the least smoke. His final choice was not very satisfactory, because the brush was difficult to break by hand and he now had no ax or saw available. Nevertheless, he collected sufficient deadwood to last for several hours, and it was only when he had made a pile of it that he realized that it was material which would have been swiftly rotted by the sap down on the forest floor. The inescapable conclusion was that the trees in this high valley were not of the sap-producing kind, or else the sap system was inhibited by the cold.

A further point which struck him most forcibly in his foraging was the almost complete absence of the vicious insects and small animal life which they had found so abundant among the forest trees. He began to realize that if they could remain undiscovered by the Pretender's men in this high pasture, they had a reasonable chance of surviving until Hilary Rounding came to their rescue. The prospect was not ideal, but it was certainly more attractive than continued tenure in the forest.

Having a fire, they now had need for meat. Bogaert pointed several sticks by rolling them in the fire and banging off the charred wood with a stone, but they were hoplessly inadequate as spears. After a nearly mortal encounter with one of the razor-horned creatures which Bogaert had attempted to "throw" with his hands, he finally gave permission for Zim to use a single ion discharge to kill one of the beasts. Zim's aim was prompt and accurate, but the whipcrash thunder rolled discouragingly loud between the mountains, and renewed Bogaert's fears of alerting the Pretender's men.

With the coming of night, Bogaert and Zim arranged a crude deadwood pile across the entrance to the chamber to reduce access to it and so make it easier to defend. Their armory consisted of the ion gun, some fire-pointed sticks, and several piles of stones which had been specially selected for throwing. Apart from the ion gun, the defenses were probably more psychological than actual. Bogaert had seen scattered bones in the valley woods which gave the impression that the carcasses of heavy animals had literally been torn apart. So far there were no clues as to what might be responsible, but the Terran had an uneasy feeling that this seemingly docile valley was probably not as safe as appearances suggested.

Having settled the children to sleep at sundown, Bogaert and Miram stood leaning on the deadwood barrier, watching the rise of the great star clusters and wondering if Rounding had yet realized Oontara's and Xzan's duplicity and mounted a rescue attempt. In a way, the arrival of the Pretender was fortunate, because this was a development which Rounding could be expected to examine with his customary insight. Providing only that the Commissioner knew that the rendezvous with the Terran starliner had not been met, Bogaert was confident the fat representative of Terran technology would deduce the rest for himself.

With the deepening of night came a chill which was only partly offset by the capacity of the rock walls to even out the temperature differences in the chamber. The conditions were reasonably tolerable but not conducive to unbroken sleep, and the children tossed fitfully because they had no other covering than their shredded clothing and a bed of grasses they had collected from the pass. Miram turned from time to time to comfort them with soft words. At one point she crossed suddenly to Bogaert and gripped his arm tightly, speaking in urgent but soft tones so as not to alarm the children.

"Bogey! There's a light!" She was very near to panic.

"Where?"

By way of answer, she led him by the wrist to where the yet unexplored smaller cavity led more deeply into the mountain. From one angle, which Miram had crossed by chance, a suspicion of dim yellow illumination was visible, apparently reflected and re-reflected by the rocky walls.

"What is it?" she asked.

"I don't know—except that, so deep into the rock, it can't be the Pretender's work." Bogaert took up one of his pointed sticks. "Wake Zim and have him stay on guard with the gun. I'm going in there to have a look."

"You'll be careful . . ."

Bogaert raised his stick to signify assent, and tried to grin in the darkness. Inwardly his thoughts were in a turmoil. If he judged the distance and the level of the illumination correctly, here was no natural phenomenon. It tied in with an uneasy feeling he had harbored about the shape of the chamber they had occupied, with its more than natural regularity. He was not surprised to find that the connecting cavities, though much smaller, were similarly formed. His theory on lava-bubble formation gave way to a speculation that these interconnecting cavities had been deliberately cut in the solid mountain by some method he did not recognize. He had assumed that the cavities were originally spherical and had been half filled by blown dust, but as he penetrated farther he discovered that where the sand lay thinner there was a regular pavement underneath.

The realization brought him to a halt in agonized shock, and he moved the sandy layer with his feet. The dim scatter of light penetrating what proved to be a corridor formed from a series of cavities enabled his dark-adapted eyes to discern dimly the elaborate mosaic of the paving, and he knew he had seen something similar before. It was the same as the paved causeway which had led from the pod site to the island. It was a sign of an ancient civilization on Avida, perhaps a remnant of an age when the dictates of survival on the planet were not so all-demanding. And in front of him—the emotion made it difficult for him to draw breath—someone or something had left a light . . .

The layers of dust and sand on the cavity floors must have lain undisturbed perhaps for many centuries, and thus Bogaert had no fear of meeting human or animal intervention. Yet the fear and excitement which inhabited him as he passed through successively lighter cells of the passageway filled him with an idefinable dread. The light was something which should not have existed, could not have existed—and yet it was there. The enigma generated an almost electrical tension in Bogaert's brain.

A staggering of the line of cells forming the passage had permitted a scattering of illumination to pass without the source becoming visible. As he passed through the last cell, however, he paused in awe at the great illuminated orb which sat on a low dais in the center of one great hemispherical hall. So large was the globe that, although its output of light was immense, the luminous density of its surface was low enough to permit Bogaert to peer into its interior. The sight was mind-twisting and fantastic, as though a complete universe had been reduced to minuscule scale and set in a glass bowl, with thousands of millions of suns keeping station in a bottled continuum.

With the greatest difficulty, Bogaert tore his eyes away from the fantastic scene and looked at the rest of the hall. He soon discovered that it was only one of a great number of similar chambers, each with a separate illuminated orb and each with the walls filled with legion upon legion of semitransparent platelets packed solidly and several deep. The realization of what he had stumbled upon brought a reactive shock that left him feeling drained and weak. Here, unless he missed his guess, was an original and major *ransad* library, and one containing many thousands of times the number of *ransad* texts previously known to exist. Such was the staggering volume of the data that it was a virtual certainty that the works continued way beyond the limits of the editions on which the star civilizations had been founded. These chambers probably contained all of the *ransad* knowledge up to the time its enigmatic creators had disappeared from the known universe. Conceivably, it told who they were, where they went, and how others could follow if they had the wit to master the lessons which had been set.

Standing before this vast accumulation of knowledge, Bogaert suddenly became aware of himself and his near-nakedness. He stood like a primitive, a crude and ineffectual spear in his hand. He felt himself to be the merest savage standing before the condensed tutorial texts of what had probably been the most advanced civilization the galaxy had ever known. Even though he came from a culture of intermediate level, he acknowledged that he was standing before the works of a master race, and felt awe accordingly.

More practically, these deep chambers would also serve as a better living and sleeping quarters for them all, and would be easier to defend. If they made these rooms their new base, he would have the chance to explore them more thoroughly, and might even discover the origins and fate of the *ransad*'s originators. Fired with enthusiasm, he turned back to tell the others of his discovery, but as he reached the entrance of the passage he heard Miram's shrill scream and the whipcrack thunder of the ion gun reverberating between the walls.

Holding his sharpened stick before him, he began to run.

TWENTY-FIVE

Once he had gained the broken rocks, Bethschant felt safer. The group of six or seven men who had started out to cover his retreat had realized theirs was an unnecessary mission and had turned back to the lifecraft. The six men determined to intercept him reached the rocky margin at a different point and had their task considerably complicated by being unable to see their quarry among the rocks. Bethschant had avoided them easily, circled back, and began to shadow them from the rear. From the direction they were now taking, it was easy to deduce that they had given up their idea of pursuit and were instead trying to find out what had persuaded him to come to the area in the first place.

Had they known Bethschant's own idea of destination was so vague, they would probably have abandoned the search at that point. Expecting to find some immediate evidence of the missing Kanizars, however, they continued to skirt the edge of the broken hills, and stopped frequently to apply their scanning instruments to the surrounding landscape. In this way, they eventually came across something even Bethschant had not thought to find: the wreckage of the powerbarge, smashed to pieces at the foot of the rock face which had halted its last despairing dive.

The shipmen's excursion to the site of the crashed vessel gave Bethschant a chance to move closer to them. From a position on a ledge of the cliff against which the powerbarge had come to final grief, he was able to eavesdrop on their conversation. It appeared that Camin Sher had offered vast rewards for the death or capture of the three whom Bethschant identified as the woman and children with Colonel Bogey. The shipmen's dilemma was that, having come across the first major piece of evidence, they were uncertain whether to report it to the Pretender and risk an entire army being sent into the district, or proceed according to the reasonable certainty that the three were in the mountains and attempt to locate and make the capture themselves.

So high were the potential rewards for outright capture that five conspirators were unanimous that the news must be kept secret for the moment. The one dissenter among the six was killed on the spot and his body flung into a crevice and covered with rocks. Then followed a discussion as to whether Hai could have captured the family or whether he had been a prisoner himself, since his was the only body found in the power-barge. They were of one mind in thinking that the remaining survivors of such a crash must have suffered considerable injuries and were unlikely to have traveled far. They made an intensive search of the surrounding area, which produced no results except that one of the party was crushed by a rock which inexplicably fell from a high ledge above the crashed ship.

Only four in number now, the group began a wider search, which was suddenly given greater impetus by the sound of a single burst of ion fire higher up in the mountains. This was exactly the sort of clue they needed, and with their instruments they began a systematic scan of the rock faces and broken mountains. They were rewarded by the sight of a slight smoke plume high in the hills and well to the left of where they had been searching. The point was many kilometers away and involved a considerable climb, which was impractical that day in view of the approach of night. The four therefore made their way along the level to a point judged to be directly below their quarry, and there decided to rest for the night and make their assault in the morning.

On these hill slopes the activity of the minor wildlife was negligible, and they were relatively untroubled by the virulent pests which so discomfitted their colleagues in the forests. Many, however, were the larger shadows which prowled around their night shelter. While two slept, two kept watch, risking the advent of more troops by firing at any and every moving shape which fact or fancy generated in the darkness. Even so, by morning one of the sleepers was dead, apparently poisoned, and their communicator pack had been torn apart by some agency they tried not to think about.

This led to serious questioning as to whether they should continue alone or return to the lifecraft for aid. Reluctantly they decided that, with their losses already so great and their communicator gone, they had better get reinforcements. High on the rocks, Bethschant grinned to himself as the party began to retrace its steps. From the concentration of their attention, he knew what their destination would be when they returned, and he decided to scout ahead for himself.

Surveying the climb he had to make, he estimated it as difficult until, experimenting with different approaches, he happened on a line of paths and steps cut into the living rock and paved with a curious pattern of even stones which must have been the handiwork of men. Bethschant had seen such patterns before, in places like the causeway leading to the island when, at the low point of the shallow tides, the mud on the surface dried and split to reveal the regularity beneath. In other parts of the forest, too, large segments of the paving were repeated, as if the ancients of Avida had laid connecting paths between places which had long since succumbed to the silent fury of the forest. Bethschant had always regarded such constructions with interest; it only now occurred to him that they should also lead somewhere.

Time had ravaged what man had built so carefully. Great slices of the veined mountains had fallen and obscured the way. Only with the greatest difficulty and with many circuitous loops did Bethschant manage to follow the route. In many instances it was more arduous than climbing his own way, but he persisted, because a swift assessment told him that the path ultimately led close to the very point where smoke had been seen in the mountain heights.

His journeyings led him to the edge of a crevasse. Here the path had been torn asunder by a mighty rent where the mountain itself had been thrust upward to leave a dizzying split which it was impossible to pass directly. Bethschant had to travel nearly two kilometers along the shattered cubic faces before the gap narrowed to a point where he could safely leap across. He then had to travel back a similar distance along the perilous ledge of the opposite face before he once again stood at a continuation of the path and was able to resume his ascent.

On a high ridge he turned and looked back across the slopes to where the lifecraft sat on a brief plateau. His keen eyesight could discern a string of figures leading away from the vessel toward the hill slopes. He estimated that they were about three hours behind himself, and if they too found the steps, there was no reason why they should not make similar time on the ascent. Bethschant therefore concentrated on climbing as fast as he could, although he found the thinning air made his exertions more tiring.

At length he came over a lip of rock and into the bottom of an unexpected valley. Even as he entered it, he knew the place was unusual. Very few of the trees were like those that grew in the forest, and many of the species were completely new to him. Grass grew in luxurious abundance, untroubled by the throttling fern, and herds of razor-horns grazed fat as though predators had ceased to exist.

Thirstily, Bethschant sought water. He found a stream, and looked around for a firebush to make ash. He could find no firebushes and no other trees which were not so green with sap that to burn them would have caused much smoke. Turning again to the stream, he examined the unusually clear water with some suspicion, then tasted it and found it lacked both salt and fleshworms. It was a new experience for him to drink flowing water from a stream, yet the novelty did not preclude a recognition of the fact that, had they known of the existence of this mountain pass a few years earlier, he and his tribe might never have been forced to leave the planet for life among the stars.

He found a tall tree, and climbed to the highest

branches, from which point of vantage he had a good view over the way he had come and could also gain a fair idea of the size and layout of the valley. Largely as he had predicted, the shipmen came into the valley's foot about three hours later, and fanned out to search a broad strip of land up toward the valley's head. The exertions of the climb had been extreme, and most had now opened their armor. Letting them draw well ahead of him, he took poisoned darts from his pouch, checked the sling holding his blowpipe, and began to shadow them silently through the bush.

TWENTY-SIX

The coming of Kanizar to Ortel was no surprise, but the mode of his coming was calculated to strike fear and apprehension into the hearts of all who dared think the Pretender a possible successor. Never before had such a concentration of heavy ships leaped out of hyperspace so close to the vicinity of a populated planet. The local effect on the continuum was shattering. It completely dislocated the pattern of weather on Ortel, causing tidal waves, storms, and earthquakes as a foretaste of the great anger of the King of Kings. A temporary time reversal ruptured every clock in the southern hemisphere, and shock waves of gravitic and entropic radiation played havoc with every sensitive device on the planet. Star King Oontara, who should have made protest against this gross violation of his territorial space, bit his lip and sent an obsequious message of welcome. The buckling of light images caused by the violence to the continuum had forcibly reminded him of his failing sight. Suddenly he felt a much older and frailer man.

Kanizar's arrival at Oontara's court was equally impressive, though much more local in effect. Instead of waiting for a ferry to bring him from orbit down to the spaceport, Kanizar landed a space-razee directly in the palace grounds. His descent ruined gardens which had taken a hundred lifetimes to mature, and generated vibrations which weakened every tower and dome and wall for a kilometer. Oontara listened to the razee's thunderous touchdown with growing dread, and feared for the very fabric of his palace. His reaction to this monstrous intrusion was to dress himself in very plain white garb and send for Manu Kan to attend him immediately. When expediency dictated, the star king could be very diplomatic.

The physical appearance of the King of Kings was as big as his galactic image. A veritable giant, his deep voice rumbled and rolled like an eternal storm, and his armored footfall could be felt as well as heard as he crashed through the palace corridors. His red hair and red beard seemed to top him with a constant flame, and the dreadful intensity of his dark eyes had quelled many better kings than the quaking Oontara.

When he burst into the audience chamber, Kanizar gave the star king only the slightest nod of acknowledgment. His salute went straight to Manu Kan, the merchant, who touched the sovereign's wrist gravely.

"Manu, what news have you of Miram and the children?"

"All too little, Kanizar. They reached Ortel safely, and I gave them my protection. Because it was Sashu's instruction, I arranged to smuggle them to Terra until you returned. It was a wise move, but one that went wrong. My Lady Miram and the children were put on a barge intended for rendezvous with a Terran starliner. That rendezvous was never kept."

"Not kept!" Kanizar's brow was deeply furrowed, and he half turned so that his scowl included Oontara in its fearful compass.

"Of this I was unaware till recently," continued Manu Kan. "I've agents on Terra, and they've only just reported. Four passengers were expected from the Ortel rendezvous, but the starliner was never met. As soon as the news reached me, I made it my job to investigate."

"And you have the answers?" Kanizar was watching

Oontara as though the star king were a mouse on which he intended to pounce. The star king was shifting restlessly under the relentless gaze.

"This idiot"—the merchant indicated Oontara with an attitude of disgust—"was manipulating the space lanes in order to trap a Terran he needed for a survival game. In his trap he also caught Miram, Arma, and Zim."

"Space!" Kanizar had not expected so dramatic a reply. "Is this true, Oontara?"

Oontara forced composure round him like a cloak.

"King of Kings, it's true I acquired a Terran champion. Whether your wife and heirs were also caught in the snare is still subject to speculation. There's yet no proof of it. In truth, I'd no knowledge they'd even landed on Ortel, else they'd have enjoyed my protection. But this merchant who meddles in politics kept the facts from me. I can't answer for the safety of those whose presence has been concealed. Manu Kan already knows I hold him responsible for the consequences of his actions."

"A good answer, Oontara," said Kanizar with slight sarcasm. "I'm glad to see your guile increases proportionately with your age. Should you live much longer, you'll be suited to match twisted wits with the Pretender himself. Now tell me where the snare was opened."

"A planet called Avida. One of Lord Xzan's pathetic mudballs."

"Ask him," said Manu Kan, "what was the Pretender's destination after his visit to Tenarensor."

"He went to Avida too—though I didn't learn the fact until he'd departed."

"And ask him," said Kan, "what steps he took to right the matter."

"Well?" asked Kanizar ominously.

"Avida is Xzan's sovereign territory. I gave the star weasel an hour to get into space to intercept the Pretender."

"And what did you think the star weasel might achieve? He runs to Camin Sher to have his ears stroked. Do you think that absolves you from responsibility?"

"Indeed not. But I'm a realist. Second only to yourself, Sher has the finest war fleet in the galaxy. I don't have the ships or the captains to stand against him. My own intercession would have meant crippling losses— which was bearable, except that they couldn't have saved the day. I therefore turned the matter over to the one agency who can swat the Pretender without suffering a bite."

"Who the—" Kanizar's surprise echoed loud around the chamber.

"I speak of Terra, my Lord. I informed Commissioner Rounding of everything which had transpired. He's arranged for ships to come from Terra, but he feared they might arrive too late. Even now he occupies my personal bark and must be close on the heels of the Pretender."

"You left the fate of the Kanizars in the hands of a Terran?" Kanizar's incredulity got in the way of his own rage.

"Was my choice wrong? Was not the Empress Miram originally bound for Terra? Am I not to learn from the wisdom of your own advisers?" Oontara sounded aggrieved.

"Confound you, Oontara! Your forked tongue talks such mazes that sometimes you nearly leave me believing that your hideous black soul is white. How unbruised your conscience must be with such a tongue for a guardian. I'll hold court over this later and examine your reasoning more carefully. In the meantime, it appears our only hope, if Miram and the children still survive, lies with your comical Terran anti-warrior."

"You can speak with him if you wish," said Oontara. Signs of relief at having deflected the ordeal broke on his brow. "The Terrans have their own FTL communications methods, which exceed those of the *ransad*. Since my bark was built on Terra, it's naturally so equipped. This"—he handed Kanizar a large pink conchlike shell—"has the Terran communicator built into it, though the setting's my own design."

Kanizar took the huge shell with a look that mirrored

his doubts of Oontara's sanity, and stared into the convoluted pink interior.

"Speak!" said Oontara encouragingly.

"Commissioner?" said Kanizar, and his perplexity made his voice come out thick.

"Rounding at your service! But that isn't Oontara, is it?" Something imperceptibly small at the bottom of the shell answered clearly, and the sound was amplified by the natural form.

"No. This is Kanizar." The King of Kings brought himself back to swift objectivity. "Oontara tells me you're en route to Avida to intercept the Pretender. Can this be true?"

"It's true I'm nearing Avida. But my purpose is to rescue Colonel Bogey and your family if they're still alive. The Pretender can be dealt with later."

"You've never struck me as a madman. What makes you think you can steal into the Pretender's camp and take something so precious from under his nose?"

"My Lord Kanizar, this bark has more tricks built into it than even the Pretender knows. If there's any sort of chance, I'm equipped to take advantage of it."

"Commissioner, you know what the recovery of my family means to me, on both a personal and a political level. Succeed in their deliverance and I'll make you the richest king in the galaxy."

"I appreciate the sentiment," said Rounding's voice dubiously. "But Terran civil servants are forbidden to accept gifts of any kind. I make no promises, because I don't yet know what I'll find. But if rescue's possible, it'll be done for reasons of humanity, not reward. However, I'll expect a better than previous reception when next I call to discuss the advantages of federation."

"You Terrans drive strange bargains. I'm afraid I never could grasp your new logic. But succeed in this mission, Commissioner, and your Federation will exceed your wildest dreams."

"Let's hope I have the luck to be able to hold you to that, my Lord," said Rounding cheerfully. "But you'll have to excuse me now. I'm approaching hyperpoint, and I wish to shadow Xzan most carefully. If I read his motives right, he'll lead me straight to where the action is."

Kanizar handed the shell back to Oontara. "I begin to understand now why old Sashu regarded the Terrans with such awe. Your part in this, Oontara, I view with much suspicion. Let's hope for your sake Miram and the children have not come to harm—else I'm liable to tear the universe apart in destroying the Pretender and anyone who was his tool."

"My Lord, I—"

Kanizar, however, was in no mood for further talk. With a whip of his heavy cape, he was away down the corridor, the sound of his armored feet making the chamber ring with unaccustomed echoes. In less than a minute, the thunderous song of the razec signaled his departure from Ortel, and later, when his task force hit hyperpoint, it did so with such casual disregard for the shape of the continuum that the Pretender could not have failed to detect the coming of Nemesis.

TWENTY-SEVEN

As Bogaert started back down the line of cells that formed the passageway, he was possessed by a more than usual apprehension. Danger had been a daily occurrence, but they had met before with no circumstance which had caused Miram to scream with such infectious fright. Nor would Zim have fired his weapon had the danger not been extreme. Breaking into the cave, Bogaert dimly discerned Zim standing in the center, with Arma and Miram behind him. All three were staring at something just beyond the entrance.

"Bogey!" Their voices sounded with great relief as he rejoined them. "It's out there."

"What is? What's the matter?"

"A creature—a shining thing," said Zim.

"Terrifying!" added Miram. Arma whimpered and clung to her mother. She was near hysteria.

"Did you hit it, Zim?"

"I don't know. It was trying to get in. I fired and it went back, but it could have been the noise which scared it. It's still out there, under the trees."

Bogaert moved to the entrance. The pile of dead-wood they had heaped across the access had been largely smashed away, and the raked ground had curious phosphorescent splashes on it. Against the nearer trees, something faintly luminous was visible against the dark background. The Terran judged it to be about the size of a horse on his own planet, but it moved in a series of swift leaps more reminiscent of an insect than an animal. Finally it left the spot where they had abandoned the remains of the razor-horn's carcass near the fire, and began to hop in its curious fashion back toward the entrance to the cave.

"It's coming again," warned Bogaert. "Is the gun re-primed yet, Zim?"

"Not yet."

"Then let's hope," said Bogaert.

The stones and the fire-pointed sticks appeared pathetically inadequate, and it was a certainty that the creature would not be deterred by such weapons if it were determined to attack. Bogaert reached out his hand.

"Give me the gun, Zim. All of you get back into the small tunnel. A beast that size won't be able to do much damage there."

"You coming?" asked Zim.

"Don't talk—move!"

The others did as they had been told, though Bogaert could tell that Zim was lingering at the tunnel entrance just behind him. The white creature was indeed coming back toward the cave, in a series of diagonal hops which took place almost as fast as the eye could follow. The indicator on the handgun still showed no charge, although the repriming time was well expired. Bogaert considered it possible that the defective mechanism had further degenerated, but he had no better hope.

The creature landed in front of the entrance, and Bogaert had a view of the apparition which had filled Miram's scream with such chill. It was a sight which brought to him a physical revulsion and an almost paralyzing horror. The creature was huge, with a white, shiny, translucent skin which reminded him of a magnified maggot or something made of white and blistered flesh. In form it was a caricature of what might have been a leopard, but it moved so awkwardly that its internal bone structure could not fit its external shape. The hideous warts and protuberances on its flesh gave Bogaert a horrifying insight into the creature's nature— it was a gross mutation of genetic animal form, something which ought never to have come to term.

This knowledge, however, did not blind the Colonel to a realization of the danger which faced him. He had no way of gauging the strengths and characteristics of this unnatural animal, but its potential for survival was indisputable. The thing seemed to have suddenly become aware of his existence, and, with breath hissing through deformed nostrils, it crouched for a spring. Torn between joining the others in the tunnel and standing his ground, Bogaert realized he had already waited too long. Before he could make it to the tunnel entrance, the creature would be upon him. He had already seen the stiletto teeth and the claws which would fetch him down. His reaction, therefore, was automatic. Although the gun still indicated lack of charge, he took careful aim and pressed the trigger.

Nothing happened. The gun remained mute in his fingers, and the horrifying beast became a white blur as it launched into a spring. Bogaert followed it into the air with his fingers growing stiff on the trigger. Then several things happened simultaneously. The ion gun fired without warning and drilled the creature in mid-flight. Blinded by the sudden light and unexpected whipcrack of the discharge, Bogaert flung himself sideways as the hideous body, traveling under its own momentum, passed over his shoulder and crashed into the center of the cave. Falling heavily, Bogaert turned immediately to see

Zim already out of hiding and about to plunge a sharpened stick into the creature's body.

"Don't!" Bogaert's cry echoed urgently. "Keep away from it, Zim. Something's terribly wrong with that beast."

"You shot him," said Zim reasonably.

"I don't mean that. See how it shines."

This was perfectly true. Now that it was in the deep darkness of the cave, the creature was shining brightly with its own internally generated light. This was not the phosphorescence of putrefaction, but a deeply originated glow which shone through the deep and waxlike skin and hinted of luminous reactions unconnected with bioluminescence. The blood fluid leaking from the fatal wound shone even more brightly. Although he could not prove it, the connection between the illumination and the creature's mutant form suggested to Bogaert a high concentration of radioactivity in the creature's fabric. Although it was impossible for normal animals to live with such a level of radiation in the tissues, there was the possibility that some creatures had managed to evolve with a body chemistry able to function in spite of it. The level was probably not dangerous to those merely exposed to radiation from the body, but it was an unknown and therefore unjustified risk to the naked young prince who presumably one day would wish to sire future rulers of the galaxy.

They spent the rest of the night in the warmer chambers of the *ransad* library. Miram and Arma shielded their faces from the light and tried to sleep while the Colonel and Zim explored what seemed to be an almost unending series of chambers containing the alien texts ascending to orders quite unknown before. Once such treasures were evaluated, the technology of both the star populations and Terra promised to take a fantastic leap forward. Bogaert felt truly humbled when he considered the sheer magnitude of the knowledge on which he had stumbled.

The coming of morning brought Bogaert back to more mundane considerations. They crept back through the passageway and carefully skirted the dead horror in

the cave. Emerging into the open, they began to gather
vegetable foods to eat until an animal could be killed.
Despite the heat of the sun, the mountain air was chill,
and in their depressed and nearly unclothed state they
felt the need for warmth. Bogaert, indeed, was on the
point of reconstructing his burning glass to make a fire
when he became aware of the sudden disturbance of the
wildlife in the trees at the lower end of the valley slope.

Cautiously he decided this activity must be a sign of
some unusual happening. Instead of lighting the fire,
they decided to investigate. Keeping against the line of
cliffs where the undergrowth was sparse, they proceeded
down the slope, staying together as a body, because
Miram and Arma refused to be left alone after the inci-
dents of the night. Thus it was that, crouching in concealment out of the direct line of the search, they saw the
group of the Pretender's armed shipmen making their
sweep up the valley.

When the shipmen had passed out of sight, Bogaert
and the Kanizars began a whispered conference about
what their next move should be—whether they ought to
try to remain in the valley or risk a descent back to the
forest floor. Bogaert pointed out that once the remnants
of the previous day's fire was discovered, their presence
in the valley would be confirmed, and this would bring
the Pretender's men to the area in force. Their best
hope for immediate survival would appear to be a descent by the route the shipmen had just used. Miram
feared there might be more shipmen still climbing, and
in any case they would be unable to survive the forest
environment without the shelter of the pod. Their situation was becoming critical.

It was Zim who quieted the discussion with a sudden
caution to silence. He had noticed Bethschant descend
from a tree, obviously unaware of the group hiding in
the bushes. The native's path in the wake of the shipmen was going to bring him moderately close to their
present position. Recognizing the native as the one they
had seen on the island, and presumably the agency who
had killed a couple of Hai's men at the time of the first
attack, Bogaert decided to risk contact. Cautioning Zim

to keep out of sight and to cover him with the firearm, the Colonel walked openly toward the unsuspecting native.

The effect, as registered on Bethschant's flat and expressive face, was comical to watch. His first surprise at finding a man standing in his path was swiftly replaced by a look of recognition, which gave way slowly to a broad grin as he saw the absurdity of the situation, in which his chosen quarry stood unarmed in front of him. It took Bethschant only a fraction of a second to detect the presence of Zim in the brush, and to become aware that a confrontation would not necessarily be to his own advantage.

The years had taught Bethschant the wisdom of taking decisive action only when he was fully in charge of the situation. With the boy in the bushes, who presumably was armed, the native was not sure of the purpose of the encounter, and was therefore wary. He stopped abruptly in his tracks, met the Colonel's reassuring gestures with a mock salute, then ran swiftly back into the trees. Bogaert called out as he saw the native turn and run, then instantly realized his mistake. The sound of a human voice was bound to attract the attention of the shipmen if they were on the alert. Swiftly the Terran rejoined the others and indicated that they had best leave the spot immediately.

They were too late. A burst of ion fire shattered the trees in their intended direction of flight and brought them to a distracted halt. Zim dropped the first shipman to run into sight, but his single shot allowed them no further chances. Soon they were facing a circle of guns, and had to stand helplessly while one of the shipmen with a communicator hysterically reported the capture to Camin Sher. He seemed well pleased with the Pretender's reply.

There was a hiatus then while they waited for the Pretender and his staff commanders to come and witness the execution. Miram and Bogaert were each tied to a separate tree, while Zim and Arma were roped together, back to back, and placed in the center of a clearing. There was much laughter from the shipmen at the ragged near-nakedness of the figures, and they concentrated on tormenting Miram by further shedding her tattered dress and taunting her with horrifying tales of how Sher would use her for amusement before killing her. Miram spat in their faces and was saved from enraged retribution only by the sound of lifecraft descending from the orbiting ships.

Among the craft which descended, one came later and fell a little distance away from the rest. From this came Star Lord Xzan, hurrying to catch up with the Pretender's party, and earnestly clutching Sher's arm as they approached the spot where the captives were held. Save for the prisoners, all the faces were full of jubilation, and it appeared that even the anxious Xzan had gained his point. Somewhere from the background, Bogaert saw the native appear and touch Xzan's hem. The star lord took him out of earshot of the party and could be seen expostulating wildly. Both roguelike faces were grinning broadly when they returned.

It was Camin Sher's jubilation, however, which really lit the scene. Years of scheming and defeat were about to be justified, and with the destruction of Kanizar's heirs he would experience the first real prospect of succession to the throne of the King of Kings. He went to inspect the children, who were bound helplessly together. He pinched Arma and made her cry out, and when Zim twisted about in violent protest, the Pretender struck him a blow which threw both children to the ground. All this was greeted by wild enthusiasm on the part of the shipmen, and, sensing that a show of cruelty was in order, the Pretender ordered wood to be cut to make a fire. The children, he said, would be very slowly roasted to death as a lesson to all who dared stand in the way of the rightful king of all the universe.

He then visited Miram and gave her a promise which made the earlier electrifying mockery of the shipmen appear a probable understatement of her fate. Again he was cheered by his men, which pleased him greatly. This was obviously the Pretender's day. He had paid scant attention to Bogaert, but when he did move in the Colonel's direction, it was in company with Xzan. The devilish face of the star lord appeared more evil than ever, and at his side the grinning Bethschant took practice blows with a long-knife on the high grasses to demonstrate his proficiency and micrometer accuracy with the weapon.

"It's indeed a day of successes, my Lord," Xzan was saying. "You've your assassination, I my execution. All honors satisfied, all prizes gained."

"You've done well, Xzan," said the Pretender genially. "Whatever you lose to Oontara I'll repay you ten times over. But all this talk bores me. Let's have sight of some blood."

Xzan motioned Bethschant forward. "My champion has special skills with a knife. He can take all the flesh off a man's bones before the fellow has a chance to die. I've seen it done."

"Then let's see it again. Because I'm not sure I believe you."

"I can prove it, my Lord, believe me. Colonel Bogey, it may please your painted warrior's soul to know you're at least going to die at the hands of an expert."

Bethschant sighted along the long-knife, which had been honed to the sharpness of the finest razor. He reached to the Colonel and adjusted his bonds so that they might not interfere with the operation. Then he turned and struck one blow—straight through Xzan's heart.

The surprise on everyone's face was no greater than that on Xzan's, who tried to register protest in the instant before he died. Before the star lord hit the ground, Bethschant had moved again, and Bogaert's bonds fell away as the native severed them with an amazing skill and wheeled again, ready to take on any attackers. All weapons had been rested for the entertainment, but now there was a general rustle of movement after the first moments of surprise. The whole scene, however, was suddenly cast under a great shadow, and a vastly amplified voice from above commanded: "Everybody stay exactly where you are. The first man who reaches for a weapon can count himself dead."

TWENTY-EIGHT

Hilary Rounding's voice. Bogaert looked up. Suspended on a finely tuned reaction drive was one of the very few true spacecraft which had the capacity to hover in atmosphere. This was the ornate and incredible bark which Terra had built for Oontara. Whereas the Pretender's fleet had been forced to remain in orbit and depend on lifecraft for planetary contact, the bark was happily situated only twenty meters above the ground, with its gun blisters manned and trained on the astonished group below.

Somebody reached for a weapon and was immediately vaporized by an ion blaster fired from the bark. A shipman with a communicator tried to summon assistance from the orbiting fleet, and had his head severed clean from his neck by a blow from Bethschant's long-knife. Camin Sher had gone rigid with an unnatural emotion, and Bogaert relieved him of his ion gun in case the situation drove the Pretender to irrational destruction.

"Bogey?" The amplified voice blasted over the area.

"Here!" Bogaert waved in case he should be unrecognizable from the bark.

"Are the Kanizars still safe?"

"I have them all here."

"Separate yourselves and bring me Camin Sher. Go to the top of the slope, clear of the trees, where I can pick you up. Everyone else, drop your weapons and walk slowly down the slope. Remember, you were never nearer death than at this instant."

One of the Pretender's men near Miram pretended to throw away his weapon, then turned it toward her. Bogaert dropped him with the Pretender's gun slightly before the man was blasted by the ship. Thereafter, there was a complete capitulation by the Pretender's men.

Bogaert nodded to Bethschant. "You're coming with us."

They ran to where Arma and Zim had struggled to a sitting position on the ground and were watching the proceedings with hopeful astonishment. Bethschant's precise long-knife freed them from their bonds with one swift movement, though it took Bogaert half a minute to help them overcome the stiffness in their limbs. In the meantime, Bethschant had darted to Miram and cut her free from the tree and was dragging her by the hand toward the appointed slope.

Sending the children scurrying after their mother, Bogaert went back for the Pretender. The man had a fixed expression, as though he were in some form of shock, but he mechanically complied with Bogaert's instruction to follow the others up the hill. As they neared the crest, Camin Sher turned back toward the Colonel.

"You know you won't get away with this, Terran."

"We'll have a damn good try." Bogaert motioned with his gun to emphasize that the Pretender should continue walking.

"My ships will blast you out of space. Rounding may have got the bark in here, but he won't succeed in getting it out again."

"Could be he's counting on your presence as a form of insurance."

"If so, he's out of luck. If Rounding attempts to use me as a bargaining point, it'll be proof I've failed. And if I've failed, there're another dozen in those ships up there ready to have a crack at Kanizar's crown. They'll hit you with everything in space."

"I hope you're not proposing a compromise?"

"A simple arrangement, Colonel Bogey. Turn me free and give me the Kanizars, and I'll guarantee yourself and the Commissioner safe passage out."

"Not a hope!"

"Think about it, Colonel. You've no allegiance to Kanizar, so why take such a frightful risk?"

"It wouldn't make any difference if Miram and her

family were unrelated to star monarchy. My answer would still be the same. Nobody who prepares to roast children alive, or threatens a woman as you threatened Miram, deserves anything but contempt. So save your breath, you make my trigger finger curl."

"I see! So this is what they call the new logic. Well, let's see, painted warrior, if your new logic can get you out of this."

Bogaert was aware that the bark was shadowing them directly overhead, the fantastic power of its engines muted to a barely perceptible whisper. This was the first time Bogaert had actually seen the bark in action, and he was more than impressed by the craft's exceptional maneuverability at treetop height and virtually zero speed. The contrast with *ransad*-based craft, which, apart from the unsophisticated lifecraft and razees, could make planetfall and ascent only from properly prepared installations, showed that Terra had already advanced an order of technology further than that available to the star populations. Rounding had said that Terra had something to sell—in both hardware and philosophy. It had only just occurred to Bogaert that both were equally important.

It was a curiously theatrical-looking group that awaited the final whispered landing of the bark. Camin Sher, his face an enraged mask, alone was fully clothed. His brilliant blue uniform was incongruous in his captive situation; he seemed like a character from a costume play who had wandered onto the wrong set. Next was Miram, the Empress, clad only in a few ragged strips which were more symbolic than concealing. With the loss of most of her hair, the toughening of her body, and the stronger, more resourceful character which had emerged, she presented a wild, abandoned figure, unashamed of her new image.

Of the Kanizar children, Arma had changed the least. The synthetics of her dress had best resisted the enzyme attack, but had degenerated to a random lace, giving her the appearance of a ragged waif as she clung to her mother's hand. Zim, clad in little more than an ion-gun belt, was the picture of youthful savagery, an image only slightly lessened by contrast with Bethschant's squat and scarred near-animal appearance. Bogaert knew he represented nothing so much as a military scarecrow. Both his hair and beard had succumbed to the enzyme sap, leaving a grizzled stubble which suitably complemented the almost complete fragmentation of his uniform.

The sudden thrust of an air cushion brought the bark to rest only centimeters from the ground. Bogaert pushed Camin Sher through the hatch first, insured that the hands that seized the Pretender would safely confine him, then saw the others safely aboard. As soon as the hatch had closed, he felt the sudden pressures as the superb reaction motors clawed avidly for the sky.

He found Hilary Rounding on the control deck, surveying the screens which indicated the strength of the Pretender's fleet above them. The evidence was that the ground party had managed to communicate with them, for the great belt of ships was already breaking into the triple units of attack formation and spreading to span not a band but the entire orbital sphere.

"Thanks for the pickup, Hilary!"

"Don't mention it, Bogey, old son. But next time you make off into the woods with Kanizar's wife, I'll thank you to leave a forwarding address. I had a hell of a job trying to find where you'd got to. Whatever you've been up to seems remarkably hard on uniforms, but I congratulate you on your choice of company."

As they thrust into the troposphere, the odds above them began to look formidable.

"I take it this is one game Oontara won," said Rounding, watching the screens intently. The matrix computer estimated the Pretender's fleet in orbit at three hundred vessels.

"Completely! Xzan got knifed by his own champion. But I'll tell you about that later. What did you want with Camin Sher? By all accounts, he's going to be a liability when we hit that ring of ships. He's another of those who has to use his worst enemies for friends."

"That's a certainty! No, the Federation want Sher for his attacks on outpost stations. His incarceration should also serve as a warning to some of the other star bandits."

"So it's a good political move, even if it's not a reasonable action in our present situation."

"Look at it this way, old son. Kanizar's set to wipe the Pretender off the star maps. If we can hold Camin Sher for trial, even Kanizar will have to admit we're a force to be reckoned with. And if we start arraigning star nobility, federation becomes inevitable."

"What's Kanizar supposed to be doing while all this takes place?"

"He's in hyperspace, bearing down on us like a galactic storm. I'm sending him word of the situation so he doesn't plow right through us. But I'm hoping the Federation task force gets here before he does. It'll be a much tidier war if we can keep the prime combatants apart with the Federation force as a buffer between them."

"But you can't seriously think Kanizar's going to let us walk away with Sher?"

"He won't have much option, Bogey, lad. He's scarcely likely to open fire on us while we have his wife and heirs aboard."

Rounding's expression showed that, in any case, the question was largely academic. They were almost within weapons range of the orbiting ships, and at such a numerical disadvantage that the odds appeared completely hopeless.

"You're the tactician, Bogey. How do you rate our chances of surviving this lot?"

Bogaert had been watching the plotting carefully, noting the size and type of ships forming the gigantic ambush.

"Very good, I'd say."

"How the hell do you figure that?"

"Well, you're the past master at manipulating incredible odds. If you can talk us through, we have no problem. Apart from that, we don't stand a snowflake's chance in hell."

"I'll report you to tactical command," said Rounding sternly. "That must be the oddest advice ever offered to a commander on the eve of battle. Nevertheless, it does contain the germ of an idea."

He motioned to the Ortellian signals officer. "Open up a communications channel to the fleet up there."

The officer thrust a *ransad* communications disk into Rounding's hand, but his eyes carried the message that the new logic was still way beyond his ken. "You have access to their general communications network. It's the best we can do."

"Fine! This is Rounding, Commissioner for Terran Outspace Technical Aid. This communication is addressed to the forces formerly commanded by star renegade Camin Sher. The Pretender has been apprehended by Federation officers and is being taken for trial. A Federation fleet is on its way to secure the area. Meanwhile, Kanizar brings his forces from the direction of the Hub. Since your cause is already lost, you've nothing to gain by remaining. I suggest you disperse and return to your home planets. I repeat, your cause is lost. You've nothing left for which to fight."

He handed the communications disk back to the signals officer. "That should give them something to think about."

It did. Although the bark was still well below orbital height, a three-ship formation of the Pretender's fleet dived for an attack. Rounding ordered their destruction, and from somewhere in the weapon blisters of the bark a new and unfamiliar weapon spoke. Almost immediately, the three attacking ships blew themselves apart, not with explosive violence but seemingly as if suddenly unable to contain the pressure of the air within their hulls. Not believing his eyes, Bogaert watched in speechless amazement as the vessels became nothing but disassembled components, all continuing their rapid trajectory toward the planet's surface.

"Zheesh! Forget the talking," said Bogaert finally. "What the hell kind of a weapon was that?"

"Called a disrupter. Latest from the Federation arsenal. It interferes with the binding forces which hold the atoms together. Anything within beam range literally falls apart. Trouble is, it needs a trace of atmosphere for ionization focusing. We can't operate it out in true space."

"Well, I don't think we'll get many more come down to us after that display."

Bogaert was wrong. Another seven ships made attempts, which ended in similarly lethal destruction, before the message went home. Then tactics altered abruptly. A pattern of *ransad* space mines began littering the way ahead. Rounding swore, and the Ortellian captain of the bark had to take swift evasive action.

"They're forcing us up to battle height," said Rounding. "Our shields won't take a direct hit from a space mine."

Building up momentum now to pass through the ring of ships in the shortest possible time, the bark leaped spaceward, with only critical control of its artificial gravity preventing the occupants being crushed by the acceleration. The attackers obviously underestimated its ability, because the first of a swarm of relativistic warheads shattered space well behind them, without coming close enough to penetrate the screens. Relativistic explosives were a *ransad* specialty not yet fully understood by Terran science. They appeared to depend on the instantaneous conversion of mass to energy and back in a continuing cyclic fashion which spread like a bubble from its point of propagation. Fortunately, it's effects fell rapidly with distance, and a ship which encountered anything after the initial nucleation was troubled by nothing worse than a violent shaking. Ships caught in the nucleation phase were very convincingly minced.

The ability of the bark to withstand the battering was soon in doubt as the attacking ships began to predict the bark's trajectory with greater accuracy. A pattern of anticipatory fire began to appear, and direct contact with a relativistic bubble in the developing phase became a near certainty if the engagement continued. Bogaert, who had been watching the screens with growing concern, suddenly smote the table.

"Hilary, fire those damn disrupters again."

"We're too high for focusing."

"You need stray ions to assist the focusing, right?"

"Right!"

"Well, what do you think the debris from those relativistic blasts provides?"

For one of his weight, it was incredible how fast Rounding moved. The results were nearly immediate. As the strange voices of the disrupters began to speak again, the throng of ships massing in their location began a strange and terrible dissolution. So savage and unexpected was this show of strength that fully thirty of the Pretender's ships were caught in the trap and literally fell apart under the pressure of their own internal atmospheres.

A similar number of other vessels were unable to escape from the area in time, and joined their colleagues in the hideous wastage. Thereafter, the bark continued without further molestation. Such a convincing show of weaponry coupled with the fact that they had lost both leadership and cause tempted none of the remaining vessels to try again. Indeed, from the pattern of ion trails it was obvious that an ever increasing number were accepting Rounding's advice to return to their home worlds. Rounding watched them go, the merest trace of jubilance on his face.

"Bogey, my old scarecrow, I think you just earned yourself a medal or two. Using their own ion debris against them was one of the damnedest tricks I've ever seen. Where did you pick up an underhand trick like that?"

"I've been taking lessons from some masters of skullduggery," said Bogaert, slapping his superior on the back.

TWENTY-NINE

There were no Terran uniforms available on the bark. Bogaert had instead to be content with an Ortellian uniform which was an atrocious fit, being meant for a star warrior of truly massive proportions. The only spare garment more suited to his size had already been given to Zim. Arma had been found a tunic, which, with the arms cut short, reached all the way to the ground and formed a curiously becoming gown. The main problem was Miram. It was not that nothing could be found to suit her, but that she steadfastly refused to have her appearance altered until she had been reunited with Kanizar. Miram, it seemed, was fiercely proud of her new image, and wanted Kanizar to be fully aware of the transformation. Rounding went to reason with her and came back with a curious look on his face, having lost his first argument in years.

"I thought I knew the Empress Miram," he said to Bogaert, who, clean and refreshed, had returned to the control desk. "But that tigress you fetched back's scarcely the same person. Heaven alone knows how Kanizar's going to stomach female emancipation. That's something that'd really rock the star empires."

"It's the new logic," said Bogaert. "She was brought up like a house pet. As a house pet she couldn't have lasted ten hours on Avida. But, encouraged to develop as a competent individual, she lacked nothing in sense or fortitude. To us it's self-evident, but to her it was a revelation."

"Well, I hope Kanizar appreciates the point, because this is one reunion where he's going to get back far more than he lost. Now tell me about Bethschant."

"He was a member of an indigenous Avidan colony

that failed. Xzan took off the last hundred or so, because they were probably the toughest race in the galaxy. Bethschant was intended to be my assassin if Avida proved less deadly than anticipated."

"That's the way the game's played," said Rounding ruefully. "But how'd you manage to win him over?"

"By happening to survive. But it was the way in which we survived that intrigued Bethschant. Watching us, he realized that, given a little knowledge and a few facilities, his own people could have mastered Avida for themselves. From that point on, we had a useful ally out in the brush."

"And to save you he finally knifed Xzan?"

"He could see that I, not Xzan, held the key to the repopulation of Avida. I've just been talking it through with him. He wants to reestablish a colony on Avida with our assistance. I can't think of a better opening for Outspace Technical Aid."

"You have a good point there, Bogey, old son. But we run straight into the problem of sovereignty."

"There's another point also. It's certain Avida once held a major civilization—I think the major *ransad* civilization. We found a library there containing *ransad* texts ranging several orders beyond anything available to the star empires. Whatever else happens, we must have access to those texts."

"That may be difficult. The star kings in this sector aren't keen on too much Terran influence so near to the Hub. They're already at Oontara's throat. I think the politics will prove too tricky."

"Not if we can get Kanizar's backing. He owes us a few favors."

"Damn you, Bogey! You're supposed to solve problems for me, not create them."

"But you'll try to swing it?"

"Yes, I'll try. But it'll take a little manipulation. In a few hours we're going to meet Kanizar's fleet head-on. I've a mind to arrange a little trial of strength."

"Against Kanizar? You have to be out of your mind."

"Kanizar won't support us unless he respects us.

What better way of making the point than by twisting his tail in front of his own fleet?"

"Hold it, Hilary! Haven't you had enough space war for one day?"

"This won't be space war. Kanizar daren't fire, because we have his family aboard. But if we refuse to stop, he'll undoubtedly try to hold us—and that's where he's due for his surprise."

"I don't see the point of forcing a trial of strength."

"Come, Bogey, you're the tactician. One day there has to be a showdown between us and Kanizar. Wouldn't you prefer it now and in this way rather than a shooting war?"

"Hilary, have you ever considered how uncomplicated the galaxy was before you decided to reshape it single-handed?"

Soon the alarms signaled that they were dropping out of hyperspace. The captain had been speaking to Kanizar's fleet controller, and a rendezvous had been arranged. From his position near the screens at the control desk, Bogaert had a fascinating view of Kanizar's task force, the pick of the fleet, as they too emerged from hyperspace and continued at sublight velocities to the place of meeting. These magnificent craft were space dreadnoughts in the most literal sense, and the bark was little more than a toy by comparison.

The signals officer thrust a communications disk into Rounding's hand.

"The Lord Kanizar wishes to speak with you."

"Commissioner!" Kanizer's voice reverberated deeply. "You exceed my wildest hopes. Not only do you bring me my family, but you deliver my greatest enemy."

"A correction, my Lord," said Rounding mildly. "I'll return your family with pleasure, but Camin Sher's a Federation prisoner who'll stand trial in a court of the Federated communities."

"What!" The power of Kanizar's voice overloaded the equipment. "Come, Commissioner—you know me better than that. If you won't surrender Sher, I'll come and fetch the star rodent myself. Stand by to be boarded."

"I wouldn't advise you to try. This is a Terran-built ship temporarily under Federation command. Our destination is Tenarensor on Ortel to arrange the transfer of the Pretender to a Federation stårship. Follow us if you like, but any attempt at interference will be resisted. Under the circumstances, your family will have to accompany us to Ortel and be returned to you there."

Kanizar's rich laughter filled the room.

"Commissioner, you've played with star kings so long, you're beginning to sound like one. But there's a difference. They have forces to back their words—you haven't. You can no more oppose me than you can get that fat carcass of yours to fly."

"We're wasting time," said Rounding. "I'll see you on Ortel."

He signaled the bark's captain to continue. The officer looked at Bogaert appealingly, as if seeking confirmation that the orders of the fat civilian could be disregarded. Bogaert reflected on the great force in their path dourly, but reaffirmed the Commissioner's decision.

"I hope to hell you know what you're doing, Hilary," he said in a quiet aside.

Their approach to the great dreadnoughts must have been viewed with disbelief. Kanizar's own amused comment was speared by a sudden note of doubt, as he suddenly accepted the possibility that the Earth Commissioner might not be bluffing. Bogaert knew what Kanizar's next move had to be, and was unsurprised when two of the larger craft sprouted bright blue tractor beams to encapsulate and hold the errant bark. Predictably, because of the difference in the ships' relative masses, the tractor's grip on the park locked in gently but solidly, and began to haul the bark closer.

Rounding waited for the appropriate moment, then called for full engine power. It was a gambit which sometimes worked when tractor beams were extended to their limits and mass differences were small. In the present situation, it was obviously an abortive move.

The obvious was wrong. Depite its comparatively minute size, the bark continued on its way. At one moment it was actually between the great ships, dragging them backward with the thrust of its truly amazing engines. Unwilling to lose their prize or to suffer more of such indignity, the great dreadnoughts began to use their own engines to counter their backward progress. Rounding watched the situation building up with mounting glee, having an insight into what was to follow.

"Kanizar's going to hate me for this," he said, undismayed by the terrifying opposition of forces which the deadlock was generating. "But he can't say he wasn't warned."

He gave a sign to the Ortellian captain of the bark, who relayed a few swift orders. The words brought to Bogaert a sudden comprehension of the Commissioner's intention, and he too was infected with some of the latter's unholy glee. As the superconductive circuits in the hull were brought into play, the tractor beams were deflected around the hull. The bark became suddenly "slippery" as far as the tractors were concerned.

Because of the great and opposing forces built up by the tractor-locked tug of war, the sudden inability of the beams to hold the bark produced the most spectacular results. The bark gained momentum like a cork popping from a bottle, while both its would-be captors, unable to redistribute the unlocked forces quickly enough, began to tumble end over end like huge cartwheels which had lost their rims.

Confusion followed in Kanizar's fleet. Primarily the ships were all facing the wrong way, and had to check velocity before they could turn. Further, they were loath to leave until their two prime ships had been restored to equilibrium. In the meantime, the bark had wound up to hyperpoint in record time, jumped into hyperspace at the highest level ever recorded, and then reappeared where it was least expected, at the edge of Kanizar's bewildered fleet.

Instantly Kanizar's voice was back on the communicator.

"Commissioner—have you any more tricks like that?"

"Quite a few," admitted Rounding.

"We've been intercepting signals from the Pretender's fleet. Is it true you destroyed nearly twenty-five percent of them singlehanded?"

"That was a mistake," said Rounding. "Colonel Bogey overplayed his hand."

"Mistake!" Kanizar released a string of oaths which made the signals officer cringe. "All right, Commissioner! You win. Take the Pretender for trial in your tinpot court. But if you ever release the star rodent, I'll move the universe to have him sought out and destroyed. And now I want to talk ships—your kind of ships."

"I'll be happy to do so," said Rounding. "But you know the necessary preliminary: an agreement in principle to join the Federation."

"You have my agreement. Prepare your wretched papers and come and join me."

"I've already prepared them. I'll bring them over, together with your family." Handing the communicator disk back to the signals officer, he turned back to the Colonel. "You know, Bogey, I think we've got ourselves another customer."

When the reunion and the rejoicing was over, Kanizar called Bogaert back, and the two men were alone in the cabin. The great king of the galaxy went behind his desk, rested his chin on his hands, and looked at Bogaert thoughtfully.

"I wanted to have a private talk with you, Colonel. I needed to know what manner of man you are. You've rendered me the greatest service a king has ever seen. And at the same time, you've destroyed me."

"Destroyed?" asked Bogaert, surprised.

"Space!" Kanizar struck the desk a fearful blow. "You're fencing with me, Colonel Bogey. You know perfectly well you've done far more than rescue my family from an ill-conceived survival game."

"I don't understand."

"I'll spell it out for you. I left a young princeling playing with mock weapons. You returned me a seasoned warrior, already blooded and unafraid. I left a son I intended should inherit the stars. You returned one who thinks this heritage so small, he'd prefer a commission in the Federation Space Service."

"I'm sorry about that, I—"

"Quiet, Colonel! I've not finished with you yet. I also left a dainty princess playing with dolls. You bring me back a tough young woman who can gut reptiles without flinching and who tells me my glorious wars of conquest are all waste and vain illusion."

"But—"

"And I left a wife—a fragile courtly ornament. You brought back to me a queen powerful enough to challenge my own dominance."

"And that makes you angry?"

"It makes me sad. Because you've proved what old Sashu, my chancellor, spent half a lifetime trying to teach me—that a way of life which was old before your history began is ending. The star provinces can't withstand your new logic. You're a terrible man, Colonel Bogey, to render the King of Kings an anachronism. Very few manage to do so much damage to the established order in the course of a single lifetime."

"I fear my Lord exaggerates."

"In truth, I believe you're a worse scoundrel than Rounding. You've abducted my enemy, alienated my heir's allegiance, transformed my wife, and undermined the pinions of history. Does that sound like exaggeration?"

Bogaert was scanning Kanizar's face, wondering how the conversation was going to end. The King of Kings, Emperor of Emperors, regarded the Colonel's perplexity with a growing amusement.

"I can see now why they call Terrans the 'terrible infants.' I really think you don't know even yet your own strengths. So let me return to you one of your own truisms: 'Adaptation is the keynote of survival.' Let it not be said that Kanizar's too old a beast to contemplate adaptation. Therefore, I'm to give this to you, Colonel. You've earned it."

"What is it?" asked Bogaert, taking the piece of paper he was offered.

"Commissioner Rounding has my agreement in principle to join the Federation. You have the second document—the agreement absolute. All my star holdings are now bound to join the Federation, and the lesser star kings will scarcely abstain for long. I wanted to give it to you personally, Colonel Bogey, because you're really the warrior who proved the star legions obsolete."

THIRTY

The trip through transdimensional space was like a long journey into winter with only the remotest prospect of spring. The occupants of the first Federation ship to attempt the crossing between the island universes were not objectively aware of the multiple dimensions of their existence. For them, relativity had imparted a comforting sense of normality. Subjectively, however, the knowledge that their life-support vessel had a length of minus nine hundred meters and its total weight subtracted from infinity bred a deep and curious dread. Only a few could even comprehend the twenty-seven physical dimensions of their absolute geometry. Even so, their journey through the googolplexed infinity of trans-continuum space was a fascinating and terrifying thing.

The fleeting but observable overlap of continuums seemed designed to do nothing but overawe and dismay. The great oceans between the galaxies, far from being unpopulated, had/did/would contain a concentration of unknown bodies so staggeringly high that it was the great galaxies themselves which appeared empty by comparison. Here were aggregates of white holes, peculiar radiating vortices, and distortions of the very nature of the lamelliform structure of multiple space; witness to universes before/during/after the creation and destruction of the universe that mankind knew; giving the lie to man's claim to a comprehension of cosmology. Here was all the terror of the most alien of alien environments—and through the midst of all this compound weirdness the lab ship *King Bethschant* was an incorrigible splint of cosmic dust which alone knew purpose and destination.

Nor were all the uncertainties environmental. Culled from the *ransad* library on Avida were advanced theorems on interdimensional drive physics which even the best Terran scientific brains could only barely understand. The resultant union of advanced *ransad* theory with Terran expertise had resulted in the fantastic hybrid units which powered the *King Bethschant*. It had been an extravagant technical gamble, and one which could have been financed only by the combined resources of the rapidly growing Galactic Federation. The results thus far had been in excess of expectation.

Space Marshal Bogaert, however, had no illusions about the perils of the mission or its slim chance of success. While nothing forseeable had been left to chance, the very definition of what constituted chance in this region of physics was itself an unknown factor. The amalgamation of the two alien scientific philosophies had introduced broad areas of uncertainty, and the entire technical crew were not only brilliant specialists in their own fields, but had also been chosen for their known ability to make brilliant improvisations and solve critical problems in radically unorthodox ways. Already many of the trim racks of equipment had been stripped down to accommodate hasty modifications to meet unanticipated emergencies. If the crew survived and returned to record an analysis of their results, not only would they have made history but they would also have taken a giant step forward in man's ability to handle transdimensional space.

The navigational and control problems were no less formidable, and were being tackled no less competently. Here Bogaert had been fortunate in obtaining Lieutenant Kanizar, one of the brightest products of the Federation Space Academy, with such a rare intuition for navigation through the unchartable that he used his instinct as frequently as he used his navigational aids, and was invariably proved correct. The crushing weight of the problems and stresses affected him not one bit. The light of battle in his eyes showed he thrived on such challenges; and his enthusiasm was fired by vaster yet less bloody dreams than those which had motivated his illustrious father.

They were approaching the point of reentry into normal space. Here they had to negotiate the tunnel effect, which should bring them out on the edge of a new galaxy far across the great divides of the universe. As they made their preparations, the tension among the crew rose perceptibly. The tunnel effect was a mathematical construct of physical domains which had no actual existence so far as theorists could determine. It was a nondimensional link between the normalities of planar space and their present trajectory at right angles to the lamellar structure of the multiple continuums. For the period of the transition, the ship and everything it contained could be proven to have no actual existence in either physical realm.

On earlier trials, the lab ships had frequently failed to emerge from the far end of the tunnel, and had passed into nothingness without trace and without observable reaction. The return from transdimensional to planar space was always the most critical direction, and this was the maneuver they now had to undertake. Space Marshal Bogaert called his senior technical officers to the bridge and listened to their individual summaries. There was nothing he could add to or subtract from their reasoning, and he was impressed by their outward show of confidence. He finally authorized the maneuver, and turned to Lieutenant Kanizar.

"All yours, Zim! Take her through the tunnel when you're ready. All control parameters are at your discretion."

Zim looked up from the control panels, a trace of strained amusement on his face.

"Time was," he said, "when, faced with critical dangers, the star folk called on the ancient gods to protect them. We know better. We simply threaten to bring back Hilary Rounding from retirement. I think even the universe has better sense than to disregard the warning."

"Amen to that!" said Marshal Bogaert.

Judging his point precisely, Zim activated the devices which caused such a local warp in the continuums that the tunnel opened up before them. As they entered it, all trace of physical phenomena outside their own frail hull disappeared, and with one accord all the external monitors failed to register even the faintest trace of a universe outside. From the viewpoint of relativity, it was impossible to state whether the universe itself had been extinguished or the ship had ceased existence while the universe continued on its way. It was a simple fact that while they continued in the tunnel, one or other of them did not exist and there was no possibility of interaction. This was the only condition in which the transition was possible.

As they sped through the tunnel, their sense of isolation grew. Apprehension was a rising tide which only iron discipline saved from turning into a panic. Many ships, on entering the tunnel, had failed to reemerge. Into what strange limbo they had gone was well beyond imagination. Whether they went into a sort of dissolution, continued their journey into everlasting nothingness, or entered a new and unknown set of continuums was a question to which they might never know the answer.

Bogaert stood by Zim Kanizar's side, watching the delicate manipulation of the controls and hoping that the brain and instincts behind the guiding fingers held more certainty of success than his own mind possessed. Several times Bogaert could have sworn that the ship was losing substantiality—that he could see through the shadows of their tenuous existence, right through to the nothingness beyond. Zim remained silent, but a slight correction of the controls each time returned the reality to the situation and fetched a feeling of solidity back to the ship. Bogaert wondered how much the impression was subjective and just how near they had actually come to fading into the negative infinity beyond.

Then, mercifully, they were through the tunnel. The instrument panels became jammed with the myriad lights and signals which recorded the return of a universe outside. Vision swam back again to the screens. They were back in real space and on the edge of a great new galaxy a million kilo-parsecs from home. The great sprawl of stars was a riot of magnificence which left the Milky Way seeming a poor lackluster thing. More importantly, they were safe, the *King Bethschant* was in remarkably good shape, and the information they had gained contained the key to traveling not only to this galaxy but to every conceivable galaxy.

Nor were the frontiers of space finite. From this new position on the edge of the old universe, it was possible to see that, far from being an ending, this was only the beginning. The cosmos truly was boundless. In all directions were limitless continuations of the scene, which left the mind humbled and amazed.

Here was the promise not of a star but of an entire galaxy for every human head in existence. Contrasting this magnitude and bounty with the smallness of man, Bogaert knew beyond doubt that the human creature had a lot of maturing to do before he qualified to master all this new wonder set before him. They now had the hardware. Only time would tell whether they also had the philosophy to match.

This was the testing time for the whole of the human species: whether it could adapt to limitless horizons. Perhaps in this galaxy—or the one after—the originators of the *ransad,* the great teachers, would be waiting. Or perhaps even they had failed to adapt far enough fast enough, and had left the challenge open.

Perhaps . . .